Dilemmas and Decisions

Maggie Fogarty

THANKS:

A big thank you to my test readers, Pip Toms, Spencer Smart, and Paul Weall. Your honest feedback was much appreciated.

And an extra big thanks to Spencer for the cover design and to Paul for his help with the book formatting.

Finally, I'd like to thank our cockapoo dog Bonnie for her love of dragging me away from the computer and out for walkies!

Canada: The Story So Far...

Do you ever get the feeling that your life resembles a feature film? A production where the director is hidden from view and the story lines are constantly moving. Right now an imaginary camera is hovering somewhere above, creating a beautifully framed wide shot of me sitting alone and staring into the distance.

The setting is a hotel room in Toronto, thousands of miles from my home in England.

It's a nice enough place, if you like mahogany wood panelling and deep maroon coloured decor. I've only been here for an hour and have already unpacked my bulging suitcase and tried out the baffling power shower.

Now there's just an hour to go before my son, Andy, arrives and we're heading out to his favourite restaurant in the Greek quarter of the city.

My son. Andy. Full name Andrew Wilson.

A boy once known as 'Edward', when he was first given a name back in 1976.

A good traditional one chosen in honour of my dead grandfather.

But our time together was brutally cut short and within a few months my baby son was handed over to his new adoptive parents. I was just a child myself, only 16 years old, and living in a strange new town in the far south west of England.

Since that momentous day I've only seen him once before, when he travelled to England a few months ago. That was after he managed to track me down through an adoption agency and following an exchange of emails and phone calls, we finally arranged to meet up.

Two terrified and excited virtual strangers linked by flesh and blood.

Our meeting in London, nearly four decades after his birth, was an emotional roller coaster of exhilaration and sadness. Laughter and tears, light and shade. Yet everything went much better than either of us could have hoped for and Andy née Edward, now a Toronto based doctor, was easy to talk to. Our time together flew by and afterwards I made a promise. Whatever happens in the future, Andy will remain a part of my life.

There is still so much to learn, so much family history to catch up on.

Yet somehow on that day everything fell into place. The secret I've kept from my late husband, my teenage daughter, and everyone else besides, suddenly standing there before me. All grown up and staring back with my eyes, yes unmistakably mine. And the rest of him showing an unsettling likeness to the father who knows nothing of his existence.

At the end of our meeting, Andy asked me if I'd like to travel over to Canada and be introduced to his 'folks' and girlfriend Lauren.

It was an offer I couldn't refuse whatever the consequences.

So that's why I'm sitting here today, thousands of miles across the Atlantic and staring out at the mackerel grey skyline and snow covered pavement below.

Wondering what chain of events I've begun, after years of living a lie.

My hidden film director shouts 'cut' and the camera pulls back. Time to refocus and haul myself into the here and now.

Chapter 1

To be honest, I knew little about Toronto before making the long journey from my home in the Cornish city of Truro, England, but I made sure I mugged up by reading a few guide books and doing some online digging. I'm used to researching things quickly in my role as a journalist, becoming a mini expert in lots of subjects. 'A cultural magpie' as my late husband used to say.

Yet getting to know Toronto as a city isn't my main priority. In the circumstances, I'm hardly your typical tourist, unless you count meeting your son's adopted family as a recreational trip. I hardly think so.

How to occupy the next couple of hours? I could try to nap but doubt if I'll succeed. Too much swirling around my mind, too much excitement about what lies ahead. As I checked in, the receptionist waxed lyrical about the main shopping mall, deep underground and already all decked out for Christmas. The massive tree adorned from top to bottom in crystal decorations was "something to see" she told me. Perhaps I'll head out and take a quick peek.

First though, I should ring my daughter Amy

who is home from university and house sitting for me. Of course she has no real idea about why I am here and knows nothing about my adopted son Andy. As far as she is concerned, I've travelled over to see an old pal from back in the day and now living in Canada.

She is aware that I'm hooking up with my best friend, Kevin, for a pre-Christmas shopping trip to New York on the way home. At least that bit is true.

It's late afternoon here so it will be mid evening in the UK. Amy will probably just be chilling out and watching some TV. For convenience I'll use my mobile at exorbitant cost and make sure I Skype call from my laptop for the rest of my time here.

'Hello....?' Amy's voice sounds sleepy as if she has just woken up.

'Have I disturbed your shut eye?' I try not to sound disapproving.

'Mum – you've got there OK then?' She has suddenly perked up and I can hear the rustle of what sounds like bed linen being pushed aside. Then a muffled cough. There is someone else in the room.

'Who's there with you?' A stifled snigger followed by a 'shush' noise from Amy.

'Amy – what's going on?'

There is a brief silence before she answers.

'Mum – you know I mentioned Ashley from University? The one you keep saying you want to meet?'

I know full well who Ashley is. Amy has been seeing him for a couple of months but still hasn't seen fit to bring him home.

'Well, I thought as you are going to be away for a bit he could stay here to keep me company. You don't mind do you?'

'Of course not' I reply, miffed that someone is in my house, sleeping in my 19 year old daughter's bed, without me having even met them.

But then who am I to judge?

'Thanks mum. As soon as you get back I'll introduce you to Ashley properly, promise. Tell you what, why don't you say a quick hello now before you tell me all about your journey?'

I don't have time to reply before Ashley is put on the phone and he sounds wary.

'Hello Mrs McKay – how are you?'

'Oh just call me Debbie and fine thanks. Well apart from being a bit frazzled from the travel.'

'I can imagine. I've never been to Canada but I was saying to Amy that I'd love to go there one day. You have a great pad here by the way.'

'Thanks' I reply, still bugged by the fact that there is a complete stranger – to me at least – under my roof. I make a mental note to get my mate Kevin to head over there later and check him out.

'Look Mrs...er Debbie, you have a good time and

I'll put you straight back on to Amy' he says, sensing that I'm not in the mood for a longer chat. Ten out of ten for emotional intelligence, I'll give him that.

I then give Amy the low down on my flight over and the hotel where I'm staying.

'When are you meeting Charlotte then?' she asks innocently. Charlotte aka Charlie was my closest childhood friend, the one who I've supposedly come over to visit.

'We're going out this evening, to a Greek restaurant'. If you are going to lie, then include at least a decent dollop of truth.

'Well I hope you enjoy yourself' she says breezily, adding that I should email her across some photos of the evening. Oh Lord, this is going to be a complicated 'legend', the term used by undercover cops and reporters.

'Hmm – I might just keep the photos until I get back, then we can look at them all together.'

Amy laughs and admonishes me for not being a social networker. I am on a work related network site but I've avoided the others – something which amuses my colleagues who can't understand my reluctance to embrace the 21st century favourite way to communicate.

'Love you loads mum' she trills, with me promising to use Skype next time. At least then I could get a visual measure of Ashley.

'Hmm maybe' Amy says, sounding less than enthusiastic. 'We've got a lot of trips planned – I want to show Ash the city and we're heading out to some beaches as well. He wants to try wind surfing if the weather is up to it.'

'Well make sure you both stay safe' I reply, adding casually that Kevin might just pop around later to pick up some paperwork that I forgot to give him before I left.

'Er - what time?' Amy asks, clearly seeing through my ruse to get Kevin to cast a beady eye over Ashley.

'Not sure yet. I'll get him to give you a call and let you know. Anyway, love you and don't forget what I said about staying safe.'

'We'll be fine mum. You stay safe too. Enjoy catching up with Charlotte.'

And with that the conversation ends. Over and out.

Never mind any thoughts of checking out the shopping mall.

Time now to call Kevin.

Chapter 2

Kevin Foster, my best mate, work colleague and a lot more besides, is amused when I ask him to eyeball my daughter's boyfriend adding sarcastically that 'at least he's the same age as her.' But he agrees to head over to the house and tells me excitedly that he's planning 'a great itinerary' for our long weekend in New York in a week's time.

I try to sound enthusiastic but I can't really think that far ahead at the moment. For now it's all about Toronto and the daunting prospect of meeting my son's adoptive family. Sensing my nervousness about the days ahead, Kevin gives his usual reassuring spiel and promises not to put his foot in it when he talks to Amy later.

'Now, just to double check - the friend you're supposedly hooking up with is called Christine, right?'

'No, not Christine stupid, it's Charlotte – Charlie is her nickname.'

Kevin titters and the penny drops that he's just winding me up. I'm the stupid one for falling for it.

'Of course, Charlie it is – as if I could forget. You've told me about a hundred times. Don't worry,

I won't drop you in it.'

The two phone calls home have eaten up most of an hour, so not long to go until Andy arrives. If it's anything resembling our first meeting, he'll be punctual like me and while I've been on the phone it has started to snow heavily.

Already I can see that my planned outfit of a cotton trouser suit with a cashmere coat isn't going to work, damn it. I've only got one waterproof outdoor jacket with me, so it'll just have to do. As for footwear, I've set aside a suede pair of wedge heeled ankle boots which are hardly suitable either. Living in the milder south west of England makes you smug about the need for proper winter boots, unless you count wellingtons. Let's just hope we don't have to walk too far to this restaurant.

Rather than hang about my gloomily decorated room, I decide to explore the rest of the hotel and pop into the Spa area to check it out. It's pretty deserted apart from a solitary elderly gent doing leisurely laps of the pool and a bored looking young girl on the reception desk asks me if I'd like to book a treatment.

'Not today thank you' I reply 'but I'll take one of your brochures.'

She shrugs and hands me a menu of treatments, adding that there is a special Christmas offer on manicures and pedicures. I can see her glancing at my hands as if to say, 'you look like you need it.' The cheeky mare.

Making my way to the bar area, it's packed out with lots of people wearing smart work clothes and name badges.

I've already spotted that there's a veterinary conference taking place over the next few days and some of the sessions are in the hotel. Everyone is talking loudly, with waiters dashing around with trays of canapés and drinks. I wonder whether I could pretend that I'm at the conference and snaffle a free glass of wine?

I'm still deliberating whether to risk it, when a tall silver haired man heads across in my direction.

'Excuse me...you're not Susan are you?'

'No, that's not my name' I reply, smiling. It always amuses me when I get mistaken for someone else and it happens surprisingly often.

'Oh sorry. I was told to look out for a dark haired lady and I saw you hovering there.' His accent is foreign, French I think, and he has twinkly mischievous looking green eyes.

'I'm taking a tour of the hotel. I only arrived from England a few hours ago.'

'England eh? Are you here for the symposium?'

'Oh no, not at all. I'm here on vacation.' I smile again, fully expecting the conversation to end there and then.

'Good for you' he replies, grabbing a drink from a passing waiter and asking me if I'd like to have one anyway.

'I won't tell anyone if you don't' he winks, taking another glass of champagne from the waiter before I can reply.

Ah well. Something I was thinking about anyway and it's not a bad way to kill a bit of time before Andy gets here. I was right, his accent is French and his name is Philippe Roux. He heads up a veterinary practice in Quebec and is here to give a talk on the latest developments in small animal surgery.

Meantime, I'm keeping up my legend of visiting a childhood friend. He's clearly inquisitive and keeps asking me questions about 'Charlie'. Is she married? Does she have kids? What does she do for a living? This is getting awkward to say the least.

Mercifully, the woman he was looking out for, Susan, arrives in the nick of time. Phew – my excuse for a sharp exit.

'Maybe I'll see you around over the next few days?' Philippe asks and I mutter 'yes perhaps' thanking him for the drink. Yikes, now I know what it must be like to go under the radar and the pressure it puts you under.

When I get to the hotel reception area, Andy is already there looking as handsome as I remember him and dressed in the sort of easy smart casual clothes that Americans and Canadians excel in wearing.

I'm clutching my bulky outdoor jacket which I drape across a chair before giving him a long hug. Eventually we break free, smiling nervously at each other.

'Debbie – you look great. How was the journey?'

'Oh very straightforward – it went by quite quickly actually.' I'm still grinning from ear to ear, echoing Andy's broad smile.

'And you're sure you aren't too travel weary to head out for dinner?' He's being thoughtful and polite but I'm far from tired now, firing on all cylinders in fact.

'Of course not and I can't wait for us to have a proper catch up.' I can see he's glancing down at my heavy coat, probably wondering why I'm dragging it along with me.

'It's the only decent bad weather one I've got' I say, apologetically.

'Well not to worry Debbie, there's no need for that. I've got the car parked out front and I'll drop you right outside the restaurant.'

After handing over the coat to the receptionist, Andy takes my arm as we head outside. The night air is not as cold as I was expecting and it has stopped snowing. Andy steers me across to his pale blue Mercedes convertible and instinctively I move towards what would be the passenger door in the UK. Andy laughs, asking if I want to 'take the wheel?'

'No thanks – I'll pass on that one' I quip, swapping over to the correct side.

On the way, Andy talks me through the different parts of the city, explaining the history and pointing out the landmarks including the imposing CN Tower. As we approach what is known as the Greek area, there are lots of specialist food shops, restaurants and bakeries. It's busy and reminds me of the Greek quarter in London where I've eaten a number of times.

'I love Greek food' I say to Andy, as the glorious smells begin to waft through to the car.

'Hey me too. I recall you mentioning it when we were in London.'

Funny, I don't remember telling him that but I must have done. I think our first meeting was so emotionally intense that I've probably forgotten some of it.

'You have a good memory then' I reply as we pull up outside what looks to be a small unassuming taverna.

'You'll love it Debbie. It's one of the top places on this side of town and does the best beef stifado I've ever tasted.'

The restaurant is packed out and the waiter guides us to a table at the rear of the room. The elderly owner, Nicco, totters across to say hello to Andy who introduces me simply as 'Debbie' over from England.

'Welcome Debbie – I hope you have a great time here in Toronto.' His accent is still distinctly Greek but with a slight Canadian undertone.

After he's gone, Andy tells me Nicco is well into his eighties but still comes into the restaurant to work every night.

'When I say work, I mean that loosely. His son tells me that he gets in the way and only comes in to chat to the customers. He's quite a character.'

I laugh, suddenly thinking about my first boyfriend, Mr DJ, who is still doing turns in Tenerife nightclubs. He's now in his mid 70s, exactly the same age as the year in which we met.

And the father of the good looking man sitting opposite me now.

If only he knew.

Chapter 3

The beef stifado is delicious as Andy said it would be and we're washing it down with some cloudy lemonade made by Nicco.

'My speciality, an old family favourite' he tells us proudly as he tops up our glasses.

Andy has to work early tomorrow so is steering clear of alcohol, adding that as a doctor he would never drink and drive anyway.

'I've seen the effects of too many road accidents to do that. It's just not worth the risk.'

I agree, welcoming the opportunity to stick to soft drinks. The long flight has left me a bit dehydrated and I can feel the beginnings of a headache coming on. Probably not helped by the large glass of champagne I've already downed at the hotel.

The conversation quickly moves on to Andy's parents, Theresa and Joe. They are a few years older than me, both in their late sixties, and have been married for 45 years. They adopted Andy after discovering that they were unable to have children of their own – apparently Theresa had a medical condition that caused her to have multiple miscarriages.

From what he's already told me, Andy had an idyllic if somewhat lonely childhood. At one point his parents did think of adopting another child but in the end, decided against it.

'I think they were worried that if they did adopt again, it might cause problems with me. I was too young to understand but envied all my friends who had brothers and sisters.'

'When Amy was younger, she used to ask me if she could have a sister – funny how she never wanted a brother' I say, reflecting on the irony that she does indeed have a half brother sitting right there in front of me.

Andy is quiet for a few moments and I can see that he's toying whether to ask me why I didn't have a sibling for Amy.

'I know what you're thinking – why didn't I have another child?' I smile across to reassure him that yes, it's an OK question to ask.

'Well, Amy's birth was a traumatic one and I couldn't face going through all that again. So I persuaded David to you know... get the snip.'

Andy is all ears, drinking in the information. Then, wearing his doctor hat, he is curious to know more.

'What was the problem Debbie – did the same thing happen with me as well?'

The truth is, I didn't really know what the

problem was with Amy's birth. In Andy's case it had gone straightforwardly, and was all over in just a few hours. Yet when I had Amy, the labour lasted for the best part of two days. In the end I had to have a Caesarean birth leaving me exhausted and anaemic from loss of blood.

'No you came into the world quickly, considering I was so young and you were a first baby. I think in Amy's case, I'd overdone things and didn't stop working until right up to the birth. Also, she was quite a big baby – a whole pound bigger than you!'

Andy smiles, looking relieved that his arrival at least was without drama.

'I think I've made up for being the smaller one Debbie. Good job I like sport because I sure love to eat as you can see!'

While we've been talking, he's polished off his large plate of beef alongside most of the mound of bread that Nicco put on our table. I offer up what's left of mine but he politely refuses.

'No – I'm keeping room for dessert. You've got to try the orange cake, it's to die for.'

I can't manage a dessert but offer to have a taste of Andy's.

'You're just like Lauren,' he says, asking Nicco to bring over an extra spoon. 'She's always turning down desserts and then ends up having half of mine. Still, I suppose it is good for me.'

I smile at the mention of Lauren, the girlfriend I

have yet to meet.

Again he's right, the cake is superb but I politely stick to one mouthful. It's lovely just to watch him eat and with all the sports he plays, he can certainly get away with it. Being so tall helps too.

We've arranged for me to meet Andy's parents at his apartment tomorrow evening.

'And we'll definitely be opening a few bottles of wine' Andy says, glancing down at his still full glass of Nicco's lemonade. This time he won't have to be at work the following morning and it seems that 'mom and dad' are partial to some good red wine.

'Will Lauren be there?' I ask as he digs into his last piece of cake.

'No, she's already got something arranged for tomorrow and even if she didn't, I think it best if you to meet mom and dad separately first. Don't you?'

It's a sensible suggestion. There's more than enough to talk about with his parents without the added complication of his girlfriend being there. Still, I'm looking forward to meeting her, especially as Andy seems to think she is 'the one'.

As we head back out into the cold night air, a wave of exhaustion suddenly hits me. It will be the early hours of the morning back home and if I was there I'd have gone to bed a long time ago.

I try unsuccessfully not to let it show.

'You must be getting really tired now' Andy

says, as he opens the passenger door for me.

'Yes, it's just hit me' I reply, sliding into the soft leather seat. The car still smells new and is immaculate inside. Unlike my old Saab back home which is always cluttered with papers and chewing gum wrappers.

'You like the car?' Andy asks, noticing my admiring glances. 'I treated myself after a promotion at work. I used to drive an old Ford and I reckoned that I needed something snappier.'

'It's lovely' I respond, adding that I've always liked Mercedes. I don't mention that my late husband used to have a 'Mercy' as he called it, his company car.

We drive back in comfortable silence, Andy interrupting it now and then to point out another land mark. It has started to snow again and the streets are much quieter.

The journey to the hotel seems quicker than the outward drive and Andy insists on seeing me into the reception area.

'And don't forget that coat of yours' he says, after we've exchanged hugs and finalised a time for him to pick me up tomorrow evening.

When I get back to my room I barely have the energy to undress and clamber into bed. I've asked reception to buzz me at 8am and I've set my mobile phone alarm as a back-up.

Now for some blissful shut eye before the big day

tomorrow.

Come to think of it, the word 'big' hardly does it justice.

Chapter 4

Despite my earlier exhaustion, I'm wide awake before the alarm call kicks in. Come to think of it, I never sleep well in hotels. There is always some background noise, people moving about and a sort of low hum that seems to pervade all hotels.

After grappling with the various shower features – there are at least six different power settings – I opt to dress for warmth and comfort, throwing on some jeans and a thick red jumper.

Rather than heading down for breakfast, I ring room service for toast and tea.

'What type of bread would you like madam?' the friendly voice on the end of the phone asks me.

'What are the options?' I reply, somehow knowing that this is going to be a long list.

I stop her when we get to the fifth choice of whole grain, adding that I'd like some jam.

'And what flavour jam would you like madam?'

Yikes, here we go. I definitely don't want another impossible choice of flavours.

'Strawberry - if you have it.' The sarcasm is heavy.

'Fine madam. Anything else?'

I reply 'no thank you' and feeling guilty about snapping over the choice of jam, I add 'have a nice day.'

'You too madam. Your food will be with you shortly.'

It has been snowing heavily overnight and everywhere is pristine white. Glancing at my watch, I can see that it will be mid morning back home.

I'm anxious to hear how Kevin got on when he went over to my house last night but I still haven't got around to sorting out my computer Skype link. Back to making another expensive mobile phone call then.

Kevin answers after a few rings and whispers that he'll take the call outside. He's at work today, sub editing the latest issue of Cornwall Now magazine, the monthly glossy publication that we both work for.

'Right Debbie, I can talk better now. You know how pokey my office is and I've got a trainee sharing it. Anyway, how did it all go with Andy last night?'

'Great – really great' I reply, keen to cut to the chase. 'Listen Kevin, I'll call you later on the computer for a longer chat. I've got breakfast arriving at any minute and I just wanted to check how you got on over at my place.'

There's a short pause before he replies.

'Well, it wasn't a tip you'll be pleased to know. I only rang about twenty minutes before turning up so they wouldn't have had a lot of time to tidy up.'

'Good. Though Amy is pretty tidy anyway, more so than me. What's this Ashley like then?'

Another brief pause, as if he's weighing up what to say.

'Oh, he seems fine. Nice looking chap, tall with a mop of blonde curly hair. Looks like a bit of a surfer dude and apparently he's into his water sports.'

'Yes Amy said' I reply, really wanting to know more about what sort of character he is.

'Look he seems a pretty sensible sort of guy and is really fond of Amy' Kevin adds, trying to reassure me that all is well. It is sort of working – but only sort of.

'I wonder why Amy didn't talk to me about him coming to stay?' I ask, thinking out loud. I'm still more than a bit irritated that she didn't.

'Oh come on Debbie. It was probably just a spur of the moment thing. You know the score, mum gone away, empty house, feeling a bit lonely. I wouldn't read too much into it if I were you. Just be grateful that he's a nice enough lad.'

As usual, Kevin's right. I'm being over protective and brooding over nothing. A knock on the door says breakfast has arrived, so I end the call saying that I'll be back in touch once he's home from work.

The tea is awful but the toast is warm and tasty

and the jam looks as if it is home made. It crosses my mind to give Amy a quick call but then decide against it. She's a grown up and needs to be left in peace – for now at least.

Instead I'll head out for a walk, explore the area a bit and perhaps pop into the much lauded shopping mall. On the way through reception, I spot veterinary expert Philippe Roux, in deep conversation with another smartly dressed man. He catches sight of me and waves across. I return the greeting before heading to the desk to drop off my room card.

Outside the cold air hits my face like the sharpest of slaps. But once I start walking, the coolness is exhilarating. The hotel is close to the university and I can see students dashing between lectures or huddled together in groups, smoking and chatting. Some of the girls remind me of Amy, oblivious to their own beauty and youth.

'Enjoy it while you can' I feel like saying. It's a blessed time of their life though I doubt few of them really appreciate it. Wait until they get into the real world of grown-ups, work and mortgages. Then they'll realise what a brilliant window in their lives this is.

The area is a mix of modern and older buildings, apartments and houses jostling with offices and shops. It's a bizarre jumble of styles but somehow it all works. Following signs to the shopping mall, I pass lots of small stores selling everything from baked goods to kosher meat. I'm just about to buy a paper and a street map when my mobile rings out.

'Hi mum, how's it going?'

'Amy darling, I'm fine. How are you?'

'Great mum. I know we're going to chat later on but I just thought I'd see how things went with Charlotte last night.'

Shit, Charlotte.

'Oh it was great Amy. I'll tell you all about it later though otherwise it will cost you a fortune.'

'I'm using Ashley's phone, he said it's fine. Kevin called around last night by the way. Him and Ashley got on like a house on fire.'

I nearly add that yes, I know, I've already heard about it.

'Oh good. I'm glad.'

'Mum – you haven't said what it was like meeting Charlotte after all these years. Was it a shock seeing her much older?'

Damn, I'm not going to get away with saying nothing until later.

'She looked well actually. A lot younger than her age. She's the same old Charlie as I used to call her, just with a few more lines and experience of life.'

Amy stays quiet for a few moments and I hope I sound convincing.

'You did say she has kids didn't you?'

'Yes two girls but they live in America.' Lying is stressful, especially as I have no idea where the real Charlie lives, let alone whether she has kids or is even married.

'Cool. I want all the low down later. You never know, we might get to see them in America sometime – I'd love to go there. You are so lucky going to New York with Kevin. He's really excited and couldn't stop talking about it last night.'

'Amy, I'll call you back later darling – about 6pm ish your time. Is that all right?'

I'm really going to have to think of a decent back story for Charlie, something that sounds pretty damn authentic.

'What are you doing now mum?' Amy replies, ignoring my attempt to stop the conversation before it gets too awkward.

'I've just been checking out the local area and I'm now heading to the shopping mall. I need a better jacket and some snow shoes.' At least I've steered the conversation onto safer ground.

'Great. You enjoy yourself. Me and Ashley are heading into Truro and we'll have a meal at that new place near Lavender's deli. They've got some great deals for students.'

'Thank Ashley for letting you run up his mobile phone bill' I reply, wondering if his parents will end up paying.

'Oh don't worry about him. He's cool about it.

His family is loaded and his granny left him a trust fund. He can afford it.'

So he's a rich kid then. I don't suppose he'll be too bothered about student meal deals.

'Well thank him anyway and enjoy your day out. Speak later and love you loads.'

'Love you too mum. Don't splash the cash too much.' She laughs before finishing the call.

Splash cash? As if.

Chapter 5

The mall is enormous, glitzy and packed with Christmas shoppers. I manage to find a suitable cold weather jacket and some gifts for Andy's parents - a decent bottle of red wine and an almond cake which miraculously stays in one piece as I force my way through the crowds.

Now back at the hotel, I find myself re-reading the latest letter received just before I headed off to Canada. It's from my first boyfriend Peter, aka Mr DJ, and I still can't believe how we've managed to keep up our old style correspondence in proper hand written letter form.

It was my idea to do it this way, wanting to keep a sense of what it was like all those years ago before the internet and smart phones. A time when things were simpler and when communications took more time and effort.

We've been writing for several months now and I'm beginning to build up a good picture of his life so far. He's come a long way from his days as a minor celebrity DJ in Birmingham, England's so called 'second city'. That's when I first got to know him, me as a gauche 15 going on 16 year old pretending to be 19. To say I was besotted is putting it mildly and in the summer of 1975 we became an item. Only my best mate Charlie knew – if mum and dad had found out they would have been horrified.

As things turned out, I wasn't the only one lying about my age and when he suddenly took off to conquer the Manchester music scene, I found myself pregnant and scared witless. That's when I headed down to Cornwall on the pretext of wanting to work as a hotel receptionist.

The first of many pretences.

In reality, I ran away to cover up my pregnancy and in the spring of 1976 gave birth to a healthy baby boy. Mr DJ's son.

The very son who tracked me down decades later and the main reason why I decided to renew contact with Mr DJ. Neither of them knows about the other, two threads of my life that have been kept separate and still might stay that way forever.

When I last wrote to Mr DJ, I was in a bad way. I'd just discovered that my late husband, David, had been having an affair in the months leading up to his sudden death. If it hadn't been for the salvaging of my old garden shed, I'd never have known.

I still haven't got over the shock. We'd been married for 25 years and he was – or so I thought – the love of my life. His death from a cerebral stroke shortly after his 50th birthday tore my world apart and our 16 year old daughter had to cope with emotional upheaval that no child should have to face. Somehow we muddled through and a move to a new house three years later was the start of a new phase in my life.

That's where the garden shed came in. The couple who bought my old house asked me if I wanted to keep it and of course I said yes. It was a memory of David, somewhere he retreated to when he wanted some 'man cave' time. If I could turn the clock back, I'd have left the stupid shed where it was along with its shocking contents.

The young couple handed me a sealed package they'd found when they were dismantling the shed. When I opened it I was intrigued – perhaps David had hidden away some old photos or other family memorabilia in there?

Then the horror of finding a stash of cards, including birthday and even Valentine's cards, all from someone called 'Jemma'. I was left in no doubt that this was more than an innocent friendship and they'd even been plotting to go on holiday together just before David's untimely death. Yours truly didn't have even a tiny inkling of what was going on.

The find left me questioning my own sanity and self belief. If you'd told me that David was capable of an affair – or if he even wanted one – I'd have laughed you out of the room. We had the perfect marriage, didn't we? That's what I believed and so did all our friends and family.

Well more the sucker me. Of course there was no way I was going to tell Amy, whose dad had been her world. But I needed to confide in someone so I chose my trusty best friend Kevin, before pouring my heart out in a letter to Mr DJ.

It took a while for him to reply, but that's not unusual. When he did eventually write back, he gave me some sage advice. His own second marriage had collapsed after he found out that his younger wife was having an affair. Now as I re-read his words, I can imagine him sitting at his desk in an upmarket English town, fountain pen in hand and some 1970s music playing on one of those old juke boxes he is so fond of collecting.

'Hi Debbie,

It's taken a while to reply to your last letter because your news literally left me lost for words. After everything you had written about David, your marriage and family life, the last thing I expected was to hear that he'd been playing away.

You must be in a complete state of shock, you poor thing. If it was possible to give you a big hug by letter, then I'd do it.

Your awful news took me right back to when I discovered that my second wife Caroline was sleeping with one of my business contacts. Unlike you, I suspected something was going on but I wasn't sure who it was with. There were all sorts of clues which I won't go into now, but finding them in bed together still hit me for six. How I managed not to physically attack the guy is a mystery to me. I guess I was just poleaxed to start with but then the depression kicked in. The stupid thing is that I really loved Caroline and for once in my life I was putting my personal life above work.

Anyway, after I got over the initial shock I decided to meet up with him. I'd considered him a good mate, so the discovery that he was screwing my wife was even more of a blow. But you know what? Facing up to him was the best decision I made. It put me in a position of power to confront him about his behaviour. It also made me realise how unhappy Caroline had been and how oblivious I was. Just because I was still head over heels in love with her, didn't mean that she was with me.

He had no real explanation of course, other than he was single and that things had just happened. It wasn't planned he told me, and he felt sick as hell about betraying me. At one point I actually felt a bit sorry for him but at least I got to know about when and where it started and more importantly, that they really did care for each other. After that, I knew there was no point in trying to save the marriage and the main thing was to make it as painless as possible for our two young sons.

In your case, you'll never know why David did what he did but my advice would be to talk to this Jemma woman once you feel strong enough to do so. It doesn't look like she's moving away from your area, so you can bide your time. The main thing is that you learn about the time scale, when it was happening and how long it had been going on. Otherwise you'll torture yourself trying to second guess. Seeing her face-to-face will probably be cathartic and give you more of a feeling of being in control.

That's my advice for what it's worth. Now to your most intriguing theme of secrets. It's a strange one because secrets should remain just that. Isn't it the whole point?

I've certainly got secrets that I'll go to my grave with and I'm sure you have too. Then there are the smaller ones, the second division ones if you like, that I might give up to the right person.

So here are a couple of little ones for you, as I do sense you are the right person. All those years ago, I think I was falling more deeply for you than I wanted to admit at the time. It was not something I was used to. I'd cast myself as a typical lad on the make, a mini celebrity who could pick and choose from any number of willing girls. You though were different. You seemed very self possessed for your age, sure about where you wanted to go in the world. A bit feisty as well from what I remember.

That was the main reason for me taking off to Manchester. I knew if I stayed in Birmingham any longer, things would get complicated. Also – and this is my other little secret – I was lying about my age. At the time I was 35, and not the mid twenties guy I was pretending to be. I was far too old to be dating a 19 year old girl and if we stayed together it would only be a matter of time before you found out.

I hope these little 'revelations' haven't come as too much of a surprise to you. Now I'm going to sign off and I'll await news of your own secrets. And how about we use the theme of our children, our hopes and dreams for them, as our next big topic?

I'm heading off to my Tenerife home for a month, so no need to rush your reply. It will be something to look forward to when I get back.

Keep positive and remember my advice about Jemma.

The imaginary is often a lot worse than the reality. Until next time.

Big hugs from afar,

Peter. Xx ☺ ☺

I've re-read the letter several times and each time it has left me in tears. I already know about his real age after reading about him a news article – I'll have to tell him that I was also fibbing about my age and was only going on 16 when we first got together. Now that little nugget really will floor him.

Then the biggest shock of all, if I ever decide to tell him. The discovery that I was pregnant shortly after he disappeared up to Manchester and that I gave our son up for adoption.

The admission that he had feelings for me all those years ago has come as a genuine surprise. I can't say it is an entirely unpleasant one either.

Still, I don't need to respond to his letter for a good few weeks and it could be that I'll stop the correspondence altogether if things get too complicated.

And suddenly the thought of what I need to face this evening hits me for six.

Out of nowhere a bewildered 16 year old girl has invaded the body of the 50 something woman who is me.

Chapter 6

Andy's apartment, just a short distance from where I'm staying, can best be described as 'swanky'.

It's in a new block with a uniformed concierge sitting behind an imposing black desk in the entrance area. When you first walk through the door it has the look and feel of an upmarket hotel, the complete opposite of my little terraced house in Truro.

Once inside though, you can see that he has tried to make his apartment more homely. Yes, there is the trendy chrome and glass and pale cream furnishings. But Andy has collected a lot of artefacts and paintings on his travels, so there are vivid splashes of colour everywhere. I particularly like the huge floor rug with its mix of bright red, orange and yellow swirly patterns.

'I got that when I went on my first holiday to New Mexico with Lauren' Andy says, noticing my admiring glances.

'That painting over there – I got that from New Mexico too.'

It's a painting of a Native American elder, his

head adorned with magnificent feathers and multi coloured beads.

'I love the way he seems so statesman-like, his wise eyes scanning the room' I observe, mesmerised by the image.

'Yes he certainly keeps a beady eye on us all' Andy laughs, before asking me what I'd like to drink.

I opt for a white wine and follow him across to the kitchen area, impressed by the scale of his open plan apartment. The spacious kitchen with its trendy glossy white units blends seamlessly into the dining area where the glass table is already set for dinner.

'This is a great place' I enthuse, as he hands me a large glass of chilled wine.

'Yes, I'm pleased with it. I can walk to work and I'm only a short distance from all the amenities. Mom and dad live about five miles down the road. They should be here soon by the way.'

I notice a montage of photographs on the wall. There are several snaps of Andy and Lauren on their travels and with groups of friends. Theresa and Joe are also on there – Andy has already shown me some pictures of them but these ones are more informal, both of them smiling broadly at the camera. Suddenly I begin to feel even more anxious about meeting them.

'They look a lovely couple' I say before taking a large gulp of my wine.

Andy smiles over at me, sensing my nervousness.

'Yes they can't wait to see you. They're also a bit worried about it if I'm honest, they are both quite shy.'

Funnily enough, this reassures me. Although I come over as quite a confident person, in reality I'm often treading water in certain circumstances. And you can definitely call this one a 'treading water' situation.

'Well they needn't worry about me' I reply, suddenly remembering my gifts of wine and cake.

'Oh – I nearly forgot. Here's my little contribution to tonight's meal.'

I hand over the nicely presented bag of goodies and Andy gives a low whistle as he takes out the wine.

'Wow Debbie, thanks. They'll love this. Dessert as well!'

He's now examining the large cake putting it towards his nose.

'Hmm almond. Fantastic choice. But you didn't need to go to such an effort – not that I'm complaining.'

He puts down the wine and cake before giving me one of his big bear hugs. He's wearing a soft expensive looking pale blue sweater and light grey chinos. Again I'm staggered by how much he looks like Mr DJ in his younger days, right down to the angular jaw and curly dark hair. Those eyes though are mine, without a doubt.

'Now is there anything more you'd like to know about mom and dad before they get here?' Andy asks, as he pours himself a beer.

'Erm, not really. I think you've given me a good picture of them and I'm sure we'll have lots to talk about once we've broken the ice. Is there anything you think I should avoid talking about?'

I'm not entirely sure what I mean by this but I suppose it's something to do with any sensitivities they might have – you know, politics, religion, that kind of stuff.

Andy smiles and shrugs his shoulder.

'I can't think of anything. They are pretty liberal minded people and have travelled a lot. There isn't much that will throw them.'

We both jump as the doorbell rings out.

'Hey – that will be them. Looks like they made good time across town.'

Andy bounds across the room to open the door, while I remain in the kitchen. I can hear their voices and laughter and manage to down a quick swig of wine before I see them striding across the room.

'Debbie – how wonderful to meet you'. Joseph, a much taller version of the man I've seen in the photographs, puts out his hand and his shake is firm and confident.

I'm momentarily lost for words and immediately Theresa heads towards me, her arms outstretched. We grab hold of each other's hands and there's a pause before we both start to talk at the same time.

'Debbie...how'

'Theresa – we finally...'

We both giggle awkwardly, each inciting the other one to go first.

Theresa is a lot shorter than her husband, softer and prettier in the flesh than her photo.

'Look there's plenty of time for all the hellos – how about we crack open Debbie's bottle of wine and take things from there?' Andy is grinning widely and waving around my bottle of red.

'Sounds like a good plan' Joseph quips, giving Andy an exaggerated thumbs up.

Theresa and I smile back at each other.

'Yes sounds like a plan' I reply, deliberately echoing Joseph.

I'm aware that my voice sounds a lot higher than usual, a sure fire sign of nerves.

As we follow Andy towards the sitting room, Theresa whispers conspiratorially.

'I don't know about you but I've been as nervous as hell all day.' She squeezes my arm and suddenly I feel like a load has been lifted off my shoulders.

'Me too' I whisper back. 'Me too.'

Chapter 7

I've said before that Andy has a knack of putting everyone at their ease and he is certainly working his magic this evening.

The talk is a bit too polite and stilted at first – Theresa and Joe are keen to know everything about my life back in Truro, my daughter, and my new job as an events manager for Cornwall Now magazine.

I suppose we're all avoiding the heavy stuff but still aware that it is coming. The proverbial elephant in the room. Andy is a brilliant host, making sure everyone's drinks are topped up and sorting out the food. He's chosen a delicious selection of Italian meats, breads and cheeses – convenient finger food that allows us to eat and talk with the minimum of fuss.

Aware that the conversation is getting a bit too weighted towards me, I steer it in the direction of Joseph - 'please call me Joe' he insists - and Theresa's life in Toronto. They are both retired now but Joe had climbed his way up the police ranks to become a senior detective. Theresa worked as a hospital nurse and they moved to Canada in the late 1970s when Andy was three years old.

'I used to go to work with mum in the school

holidays' Andy says, smiling across at Theresa. 'They had a playgroup at the hospital for us kids and I loved seeing the doctors and nurses whizzing around in their white coats and uniforms. I think that's why I became a medic.'

'But no interest in policing' Joe observes, laughing and raising his eyes to the ceiling.

'I think I'd have made a lousy detective dad' Andy replies, pouring himself another wine before checking if we need a refill. We've all been so busy talking that our wine glasses are still full.

'I might have over done it on the drinks front' Andy quips, shrugging his shoulders and moving across to sit next to me. It's a reassuring move and I love him for it.

There's more increasingly relaxed chit chat and cooing over the lovely food, before Andy announces that he's going to make some proper coffee to go with the cake I bought.

'Tell you what – how about dad and me load the dishwasher and leave you two by yourselves for a bit?' Again a thoughtful gesture to allow me and Theresa to talk about the real topic we want to get onto.

Andy's adoption and our reunion after all these years.

As soon as Andy and Joe have moved out of earshot, Theresa wastes no time.

'I can't say how delighted I am that you

answered Andy's letter and have finally got to meet him – and us of course.' She moves across to sit alongside me, bringing what is left of my wine gift with her.

'Me too' I reply, nodding as she gestures to top up my glass.

We both take a sip before continuing.

'You know, I was always totally honest with Andy about his adoption from a very early age. At first he asked me questions about England, who his birth mom and pop were and he even asked me once whether I thought he had a brother or sister.'

Theresa's voice is soft like Andy's but she still has the trace of a sing-song Liverpool accent. Both she and Joe had originally come from the city and they were still living in the area when they adopted Andy. It explains why the woman from the Merseyside adoption agency – the one I've nick-named 'Liverpool Lil' – got in touch.

'It's good that you told him the truth from the start' I reply, mentally contrasting her approach with my own one of secrecy and deception.

'Can I ask you something Debbie? Do you ever regret not telling your family?' Her tone is kindly, non-judgemental but still curious.

I take another large sip of wine before replying.

'Andy has asked me the same question. As a kid myself when he was born, the only way out I could see was to hand him over to what I hoped would be good parents and to try to move on with my life. There was no way I could tell mum and dad – dad was ill at the time and the shock would have killed him.'

'And what about your husband...?' Theresa is scanning my face for any signs that she might be pushing too far with her questioning. I give a half smile to show that I'm fine to carry on.

'Once I hid it from my family, I thought it was best to keep it that way. I suppose I was worried that David might let something slip. After a while life just got in the way and holding onto my secret just seemed to be the right thing to do.'

'And was it the best thing for *you* Debbie?' She emphasises the 'you' to make her point.

This is a difficult one to answer truthfully. To some extent it was the right thing for me back then, even though I was motivated by the fear of upsetting my family. Yet, as I sit here today, with my son and his adoptive parents, I'm left wondering whether it really was the best decision.

'Now that I've met you all, I'm not really sure' I reply, feeling my eyes welling up.

Theresa takes hold of my hand, squeezing it gently.

'You had to do what felt was right at the time and sometimes, you know, keeping things to yourself can be better than telling all. It's just that it must have been such a burden for someone so young.'

I nod, desperately trying not to burst into tears. Sensing my discomfort, Theresa moves the conversation onto less tricky territory.

'You know Debbie, we are so privileged to have Andy in our lives. We couldn't have hoped for a better son but I have always been aware that our luck was your sacrifice. That's why it is so great to finally get to meet you.'

We both stay silent for a few moments, contemplating how our lives have become inextricably linked and will be for the rest of our days.

'Sometimes I did wonder where Andy – I called him Edward then – was living, what he was doing and how his life had turned out. Not all the time but certainly on birthdays and times like Christmas.'

Theresa is listening but also seems deep in her own thoughts.

'Yes, I also thought about you too Debbie. How you were doing, did you have any other children and...were you asking the same things...'

This last bit is as much a question as a statement. The subtext is clear – did I ever think of contacting Andy before he took the decision to approach me?

There's an awkward silence before I can answer.

'Although I thought about him, I never contemplated trying to get in touch. I hope that doesn't sound harsh but I couldn't risk my secret coming out.'

We are both aware of the irony of this, now that I'm sitting in Andy's living room and thousands of miles from home.

'Yet you did reply to Andy's letter, which is amazing. I tried to prepare him for some bad news – that you might not want anything to do with him....'

Theresa glances across to gauge my reaction, wondering yet again if she has caused any offence. Of course she hasn't.

'Yes, it might seem odd but the fact that he approached me first changed everything. It wasn't me initiating contact and I quickly sensed that he wasn't pushing for me to reveal anything to my family. It was just so lovely to meet him without any pressure.'

Theresa nods, taking another sip of her wine.

'I must say Debbie you have good taste in wine. This is delicious.'

We both smile, conscious that we've only got a few more minutes before Joe and Andy wade back in.

'I couldn't have hoped for a better mum and dad for Andy' I say truthfully, raising my glass to her.

We clink our glasses, two mothers cementing a relationship that didn't really exist just a few hours ago.

'One thing Debbie, before the boys come back. Have you ever wondered about Andy's father, who and where he might be?'

Her question throws me and I can feel my face reddening. Jeez, how to answer?

'No not really. I didn't even know who he was I'm ashamed to say. It was my first time at a party, I had too much to drink and well....'

We both flinch as Andy and Joe stride into view, carrying a large coffee pot and cake laden plate between them. In the event, their timing is impeccable.

'Right then mom, do you want to do the honours?' Andy is brandishing a cake knife, waving it in our direction.

And with that we both glance over, responding to his word 'mom'.

'Tell you what, you make the first slice Debbie' Theresa replies, diplomatically avoiding any awkwardness.

'Oh no, it has to be you' I insist, touching her arm to reinforce my wish.

Again we exchange smiles and Theresa gives me a small wink.

Our one-to-one chat is nowhere finished.

But right now I'm more than relieved to have a change of subject.

Chapter 8

Over coffee, the conversation reverts back to the lighter topic of Toronto's weather and plans for Christmas. If they are wondering about my relationship with 'my friend' Kevin, and the fact we are taking a pre-Christmas break in New York, they are much too polite to say.

It's now Theresa's turn to help Andy with the remaining washing up. A chance to have a private chat with Joe, something I expect has been pre-planned. I don't mind though, even if it means revisiting some of the things I've been discussing with Theresa.

In the event, Joe's questions are far more wide-ranging and he seems especially interested in my mother and sister.

'How do you think they'd react if you were to tell them?' he asks, after I've put him in the picture about mum living with little sister Carol and her husband in Wales.

It's been something that has occupied my mind ever since I decided to make contact with Andy. Let alone the consequences of telling Amy.

'Truthfully, I don't really know. We're in touch

regularly and I do travel to Wales every few months to see them. Mum is quite frail now and doesn't go out much. I think after the shock, they'd be angry and hurt.'

Joe stays quiet, a skill of a good interviewer. I can see he must have been an ace detective, teasing information out gently but methodically.

I feel obliged to fill the gap.

'The real one I'm worried about is Amy. I think I could cope with mum and Carol's reaction - well just about. But the thought of hurting Amy is something which scares the hell out of me.' Just thinking about it has brought me back to the verge of tears.

'I can well understand that' Joe replies, keeping his kindly hazel eyes fixed on me.

'The thing is Debbie, you must only do what you want to do. There will be no push for anything to happen from this end. We're just delighted to have met you and if that's where things stay, then so be it.'

He smiles across and I can see that he means it. I've only spent a few hours in Joe and Theresa's company but already I know that I like them a lot. I can see where Andy has developed his easy going personality and that there is a huge amount of love between them. If I could have devised the best possible parents for my son, they would be it. Period.

'Thanks Joe. I know that I can trust you all. It's

not going to be easy deciding what to do.'

'Of course it isn't Debbie. As long as you know that we'll be here whatever the choice you make.'

For Joe it's all about the present, whereas my talk with Theresa was much more rooted in the past. Talking to them has been cathartic – the very word used by Mr DJ in his last letter - and the only awkward moment was when Theresa mentioned Andy's father. It feels rotten deceiving them about Mr DJ, but in the circumstances what other choice do I have?

'Now then, how about we make plans for the rest of your time here?' Joe says, moving the conversation on to more cheerful matters. I get the impression that he is one of life's optimists, despite some of the horrors he must have seen in his time as a policeman.

'What's this I hear about plans?' Andy asks, as he strolls back towards the sitting room area, Theresa following.

'I was just suggesting that we come up with some ideas for Debbie during her stay. What do you reckon?' I notice an exchange of glances between him and Theresa and I suspect they've already got a game plan in mind.

'Debbie fancies a trip to Niagara Falls, don't you?' Andy replies as he moves across to fill up my wine glass. To hell with it, I'm going for an extra glass of red.

'Thanks Andy. Yes, Niagara's a definite and also

the CN tower.'

'So not scared of heights then?' Joe quips, gesticulating to Andy that he also wants his glass refilled.

I laugh, shaking my head.

'No. Unless you count going up ladders. It took me years before I plucked up the courage to go into the roof loft of my old house.'

I smile at the image of myself teetering up the loft ladder to retrieve some remnants of my old life. Including the teenage diary I kept back in 1975. Overcoming a fear of heights to connect with the past, seems such a long time ago now. Yet it was barely twelve months ago - and boy what a year it has turned out to be.

'Yes, I remember those old roof spaces' Theresa says, sitting herself down beside me. 'When we cleared out my dad's house, it took weeks to shift his loft stuff.'

'What about the reindeer head he had hidden up there?' Joe laughs which is his cue to tell the story about how Theresa's dad had acquired the huge relic from a pub that had closed down.

'Tell Debbie what you did with it.' Andy smiles and I can see that the story has been recounted a number of times over the years.

Theresa picks up on the tale.

'We took it to a car boot sale. Someone bought it for £20, a small fortune at the time. Last we saw of it, the head was poking out of the side window of the guy's mini car. I swear it had a grin on its face.'

They all giggle, me included. Suddenly I realise that there is a whole new family history to come to grips with, the Wilson side of the family.

Mr and Mrs Wilson and their adopted son Andy. My long lost boy.

Joe and Theresa offer to take me to visit Niagara later in the week.

Meantime, Andy wants to show me the CN Tower tomorrow afternoon and to introduce me to his girlfriend Lauren.

'You'll like Lauren' Joe says, glancing over at a framed picture of her on the wall. 'She's a beautiful person inside and out.'

The photo looks as though it has been taken at a professional studio. Lauren is stunning looking with long strawberry blonde hair and almond shaped green eyes. She has pale flawless skin and the camera loves her.

'Brains as well as beauty' Theresa adds, smiling across at Andy. The message is clear. They definitely approve of Lauren.

Whether it's the copious wine or the emotion of meeting Andy's parents, I suddenly feel wiped out. Ever observant, Andy suggests that he sorts out a taxi for me.

'Nonsense, you can share ours' Joe says, digging out a battered taxi card from his trouser pocket.

As we make our way back down to the lobby, I catch a reflection of the four of us in the huge glass door heading to the outside world.

Theresa, Joe and Andy are walking behind me. They look happy and relaxed. As for yours truly, the best image that comes to mind is of a wild creature caught in a headlight.

Dazed and bemused.

Perhaps that's what finally did for the poor reindeer whose head was found in Theresa's dad's house.

The thought makes me smile. Inwardly at least.

Chapter 9

Alone again in my hotel room, I'm back to being wide awake and mulling over the evening.

It had gone well, better than I could have hoped for. During the taxi journey back, Theresa even suggested that I might stay over at their place for a night or two.

'We've got plenty of room' she added as Joe nodded approvingly.

It's a kind suggestion, but I'm not sure whether I'm ready for that amount of shared intimacy just now. Perhaps next time – if there is one.

I'm not in the mood to call home yet either. Amy will be full of questions about my mythical long lost friend Charlie and her fictional family. Then I'll have to make small talk with Ashley, having spent the entire evening getting to know two strangers. No, that conversation can wait until tomorrow.

Kevin, on the other hand, should be home now and with Skype up and running I'll be able to catch sight of him as well.

It takes a while for him to respond.

'Debbie, sorry about the wait. I was in the

shower. Hang on a mo while I sort out the camera this end.'

When he comes into view his hair is flattened and he's wearing a tatty looking dressing gown. Still, it's great to clap eyes on him, even if the camera shot is pretty ropey.

'So how did it all go?' Kevin being Kevin, cuts straight to the point. That's one of the things I love about him.

'Great. Really great. Theresa and Joe are lovely people and Andy has been an amazing host. '

'Go on then. Spill a bit more.' Kevin has cocked his head to one side like he always does when he's concentrating.

'Well I managed to have a chat with Theresa and Joe on their own which was good. She asked me a lot of questions, mainly about keeping everything a secret for all these years. Then she asked me if I ever wondered about who Andy's dad was.' I clear my throat as I recall this most awkward of questions.

'Hmm – I bet you were thrown by that one. How did you get round it?' He reaches across the screen and suddenly the camera focus becomes clearer. Then he moves closer towards the screen and it feels as though he is sitting just across the room rather than thousands of miles away. The wonders of technology.

'I just repeated my story about not knowing, being drunk at my first grown up party. Then Andy saved the day by walking into the room at exactly the right time.'

'What about Joe?' Kevin runs his fingers through his sodden hair, the dampened curls making him look younger and more vulnerable.

'Oh, he was more interested in Amy and my mum and Carol. How they'd react if I were to tell them.'

Kevin stays quiet for a few moments and shifts on his seat.

'Well, that's the really tough question. Did he suggest how you should move forward?'

'No, quite the opposite. He said that there would be no pressure from any of them for me to tell my own family. They are just pleased to have met me.'

Out of the corner of my eye I can see a small red light flashing on my hotel phone, showing that someone has left a message. It must have been there when I got in but I haven't noticed it up to now.

'Well that's good then Debbie. What else did you talk about?'

I give him a few nuggets about Theresa and Joe, and tell him about our plans to visit Niagara Falls.

He gives a low whistle.

'Lucky you. I'd love to go there. Still we've got New York to look forward to. Now on that score...'

He starts to reel off a list of places we should go to but I'm only half listening. That red light keeps winking across at me and it's bloody irritating.

Kevin can see I'm distracted.

'Hey – it's getting late your end, so I'll email you my New York thoughts. You've got enough on your plate for the next few days.'

'Sorry Kevin. I've still not adjusted to this time zone and I'm only half with it to be honest. How about we chat again tomorrow after I've met Andy's girlfriend?'

He nods, smiling down the camera and blowing a kiss. I wave back at him and we call it a day.

Immediately I reach across and press the answer phone switch on the hotel phone. I'm half expecting it will be Andy wishing me good night.

But I'm taken aback by his voice with its marked French accent.

'Hi it's Philippe Roux here. We met at the hotel bar the other day. I hope you don't mind, but I got your room number from reception and I was just wondering if you'd care to join me for a drink? I so enjoyed our chat and it would be nice to meet up with you again. I'm in room 515 and I'll be around for another three days. Not to worry if you don't want to, I promise I won't take offence. Hope you are having a nice vacation and that you are enjoying seeing your friend.'

Well, I certainly wasn't expecting that. He's a nice enough guy with an interesting job but go for a drink with him? It might be an innocent gesture, a kindly old gent wanting to get away from his colleagues for an evening.

Then again....

Hell's bells.

Chapter 10

Having finally nodded off like a baby, I make my way down to breakfast keeping an eye out for any sign of Monsieur Roux. After sleeping on it, I've decided to take up his invite for a drink. After all, I'm a grown up woman and can handle myself. What's the harm in joining an entertaining older gent for a friendly chat?

In my mind I can hear Kevin's tongue-in-cheek response.

'Well you do have a track record with the older ones Debbie.'

There's no sign of Philippe in the restaurant, so I scan the local paper while digging into my delicious smoked salmon and scrambled eggs. The main news story is a poignant one about a young man who took his own life by jumping off the top of a multistorey car park. His girlfriend had just dumped him and he left behind a note saying that he couldn't live without her.

There's an interview with his distraught parents and younger sister, saying what an amazingly talented young man he was and how he had his whole life ahead of him. He was only 20, just a year older than Amy and looks even younger in the photo accompanying the article.

I try to imagine what that poor family is going through. Any sudden death is awful, as I well know. But suicide takes things to another and even more painful dimension.

My mind flicks back to one of my first stories as a trainee news reporter on the weekly Echo newspaper. It was about a middle aged doctor, a great GP by all accounts, who took a drugs overdose in his own surgery. No one could understand why. He apparently had a happy family life and was well thought of by all his patients. A healer unable to heal himself, and the story touched me deeply.

I toss the paper to one side, trying to put this saddest of stories out of my mind. The sun is streaming through the restaurant window and I fancy doing a bit more Toronto exploration today, ahead of my late afternoon outing with Andy and his girlfriend.

But first I'll need to leave a message for Philippe to arrange when and where we'll meet.

Passing the reception desk, I ask the smartly uniformed young man behind the counter to put me through to room 515.

'Hello Philippe speaking' he replies briskly.

'Hi it's Debbie here. You left a message for me yesterday...'

'Ah, Debbie. Thank you for ringing back.' He pauses for a moment, as if he's trying to second guess my response.

'Thanks for inviting me for a drink, it's very kind of you. I'd love to take you up on it.' Inwardly, a little voice is telling me that I hope I'm doing the right thing.

'Oh great. How are you fixed for this evening?'

' I'm going out with some friends to the CN Tower later this afternoon and I think we'll have an early dinner. So I probably won't be back here until after 9pm.'

'That sounds perfect for me. I'm giving a talk at 7pm and by the time that finishes, I'll be in need of a drink and a chat about anything other than veterinary practices.'

He laughs, adding that he has spent the past few evenings trying to avoid some of his fellow conference goers.

'Yes, I've been to similar professional gatherings and I know what you mean. After a day of listening to your colleagues spouting on, you just need to unwind.' As I say this, a dapper young man glances over in my direction. Whoops – I should really keep my voice down.

It's funny, but back in England I wouldn't dream of hooking up with a total stranger for a social drink – unless it was linked to work. But in a foreign country, well to hell with it.

'Fantastic Debbie. I'll be in reception for 9pm and we'll go to a little wine bar I know just around the corner. Hopefully there won't be any other conference bods there – if I spot anyone we'll make a sharp exit.'

He laughs again, like a naughty schoolboy planning to bunk off school. It strikes me that he sounds much younger than his age, which according to my earlier internet search on him is 68 years. Not that much younger than Andy's real dad, Mr DJ.

'Fine. I'll see you later then Philippe. Good luck with the talk.'

'Ah I can do that standing on my head' he jokes, adding that he thinks I'll enjoy my trip to the CN Tower.

So that's that then. My first Canadian date, if you can call it that. I wonder what Amy would make of it?

Talking of Amy, I need to make a few notes about my supposed mate Charlie before I start my excursion. A 'back story', as a dramatist might say. Or a 'legend' if I was working as an undercover reporter. Not that I've ever done that. The budgets on the Echo would never stretch to anything investigative.

There's a small public garden area near the hotel and it's where I've chosen to make up my 'Charlie' story. I'm sitting on a bench surrounded by groups of students, joggers and dog walkers. It is cold but the sun is still shining and despite the activities going on all around, the place still has a peaceful feeling to it. A small oasis in the bustling city.

So then, how am I going to create your life Charlie? I've already given Amy the impression that I've got the basics from you. Married, now divorced and with two girls in their twenties both living as students in Florida. Names for the girls? I always remember that Charlie liked the names Becky and Tracie, so they'll do. And the estranged husband? I'll call him Nick Smyth, after an old newspaper colleague.

What's Charlie's job? I could make things easy by pretending that she had always been a stay-at-home mum. But despite the pretence, I'd like her story to feel authentic and I somehow think Charlie would have a job. So I'll make her a private tutor, teaching English which was her best subject at school.

Next – her house. I'll go for one of those older sprawling properties on the outskirts of the city and looking around at all these dog walkers, I'll also give her a pet pooch. Charlie grew up with a family dog, so that fits well. She used to have a cocker spaniel called Mel, so I might as well give her the same breed. Yes, a little roan cocker spaniel also named Mel – as I've said before, always have a good dollop of truth in your myth. It helps jog the memory.

I'm now trying to imagine what Charlie would look like, nearly four decades down the line. She would be quite short as she was back then, and her hair would still be fine. But today, she'd have a sleeker Bob cut with highlights to disguise the grey.

Somehow I think Charlie would be into physical fitness, so I'll make her a keen jogger, lean and mean.

Of course Amy will demand to see photos. That's going to be the tricky one to deal with. In previous times I could have pretended that I'd had my camera stolen and lost them all. That was before the days of social media though, when everything can be down loaded with ease.

The only answer would be to photograph someone who looks a bit like my mythical Charlie, which won't be easy. Or I could to pretend that yes, I've lost my camera and that Charlie is doing up a commemorative photo album of my trip. Kicking the can down the road I know, but Amy might just about buy that one. Especially if I joke that Charlie is as much as a social media refusnik as me.

'Mind if we sit here?' A young woman accompanied by a huge Husky type dog, is standing alongside me. She's clutching a giant cup of coffee which smells divine.

'Be my guest' I reply, closing my notebook. 'I'm just about to go in search of a coffee myself.'

She plonks herself down, gesturing to her dog to sit at her feet. It does so immediately, so clearly a well trained mutt.

'You a visitor?' she asks, looking at my notebook.

'Yes' I reply, 'I'm visiting from England.'

We pass a few minutes in idle chit-chat before I

take her advice, and head towards a large white kiosk selling coffee and snacks. It's clearly as good as she says, because there's a gaggle of student types hanging around and a long queue waiting to be served.

I quick check of my watch shows that it will be safe to ring Amy. Might as well do this while I wait for the queue to subside.

So here goes. 'Mythical Charlie', you are about to be introduced to my daughter.

Compared to what I'm already keeping from her, surely a few more little white lies are neither here or there?

That's my phony logic anyway.

Chapter 11

'Mum – let me ring you back to save your phone bill. Ashley doesn't mind if I use his phone.'

I don't have time to protest before Amy ends my call and within a few minutes calls me back.

'I hope Ashley is fine with this Amy. I don't think we should take advantage.'

Amy laughs, telling me to take a 'chill pill' and insisting that Ashley really doesn't have a problem.

'He phones his dad in Australia all the time mum.'

Australia? I don't remember Amy saying anything about his dad living over there. Or Ashley having a trust fund from his grandmother, come to think of it. There is so much I still need to learn about this boyfriend of hers.

'What is his dad doing in Australia?' I ask, trying to keep the surprise from my voice.

'He works for a big bank in Sydney. Him and Ashley's mum split up a few years ago. Ashley's older sister, Davina, lives out there with him. Ashley's a mummy's boy though.'

I can hear a guffaw in the background and Amy

giggles mischievously.

'Well I still think we shouldn't overdo the calls on his phone. Say thanks for me.' I hear Amy mouthing that 'mum says thanks' and a 'Hi Mrs McKay' being shouted back from Ashley.'

'So mum how's it all going?'

With my Charlie myth in place, it's surprisingly easy to give Amy the impression that our reunion is going well. Even my physical description of her has an authentic ring to it.

'Sounds great mum. Do you think she'll visit us in Truro?'

'Maybe' I reply, a bit too quickly. 'It's a long way though, and she's always busy with her private students.'

Amy, quite rightly, isn't buying this one.

'Oh she must take holidays sometimes mum. And if she stays at our place, it won't be that expensive. I'd love to meet her.'

'Well we'll see' I snap, deftly changing the subject onto my planned visit later to the CN Tower.

'Cool mum. Make sure you take loads of pictures. I wish you'd get yourself on a proper social networking site. Me and Ashley can't believe what an information dinosaur you are.' She laughs and I can hear Ashley joining in.

'Maybe I'll get around to signing up to one. It just seems like a bit of a waste of time to me'.

Who cares what someone is having for their dinner or what latest pop psychology they want to pass on?

That kind of day-to-day minutiae used to be confined to diaries, like the one I kept as a teenager and like the one I'm keeping now. Something for me to look back on and not necessarily to be seen by anyone else. Why does everyone have to share their lives with half the sodding world anyway? I just don't get it.

'But you can download photos and give updates on your trip' Amy replies, obviously not understanding my objection.

Time to change the subject again.

'Do you want to put Ashley on so I can say thanks in person?' I ask, noticing that the coffee queue has dwindled and not wanting to rack up Ashley's phone bill any longer.

'OK. I'll catch up with you later. Here's Ashley – love you mum.'

'You too darling.' Amy passes the phone to Ashley, who seems a bit sheepish when he gets on the line.

'Hi Mrs McKay, sorry I mean Debbie. Sounds like you are having a great time in Canada.' He pauses, waiting for me to fill the void.

'Yes I am Ashley. Now, you are definitely OK about Amy calling me on your mobile phone? '

'Of course I am Mrs ... Debbie. I'm always

ringing abroad and have a good deal with them. You're more than welcome.'

His voice has a slight south west country lilt to it but otherwise it is hard to detect a definable accent. It's a sort of posh neutral but not unpleasant.

I tell Ashley that I'm looking forward to meeting him properly when I get back and he says politely that he's 'defo keen' to meet me too.

'You've got an ace den Debbie – I like older houses. They've got so much more about them than newer ones haven't they?'

I agree, not sure whether he's just over egging the politeness or really means what he's saying.

'Er by the way – Amy says can you bring back some proper Maple syrup?' he adds, as Amy makes silly hand clapping noises in the distance. She's done that since she was a toddler, usually at the prospect of getting something yummy to eat.

'Of course' I reply, asking if he'd like me to bring anything back as well?

The question seems to throw him but after a few seconds he says that he'd like a T-shirt.

'Anything as long as it screams out Canada' he says and I promise that I'll get him one.

And we leave it there. Time now for that coffee and a saunter around Toronto.

The Harbourfront area is where I head to first and I spend some time rooting around the antique market. I can't resist buying a couple of old photographs of the area, showing what it was like before it became the sophisticated spruced up place it is today. I'll hang those alongside my photos of 19th century Truro which I've got in my little 'office-cum-spare-bedroom' back home.

Then I opt for a boat tour which gives some dazzling views of downtown Toronto.

Although I'm enjoying the sights, it's not the same without a companion to share the experience with. Kevin would love this. So too would David, and I can feel a wave of sadness wash over me as this thought springs to mind.

David, my now dead husband.

David who was much loved.

David who was having an affair just before he died.

Oh David, what have you done to my memories of you?

Although both tired and exhilarated from my explorations, I need to gear up for my first meeting with Andy's girlfriend. Everyone has told me what a lovely person she is but for some reason I feel uneasy.

In my job as a magazine events manager, I'm meeting new people all the time. And I've already jumped two huge hurdles, in making contact with my adopted child and the parents who made him their own. So meeting Lauren should be a doddle.

I can sense already that she will become part of my new extended family and that her and Andy might even have their own kids one day.

My grand children. Jeez, as Kevin would say, it's quite a thought and that could explain why I've got qualms about later today.

So I'll do what I usually do when my confidence needs a boost. Get dolled up to the nines, put on some warpaint and a killer pair of heels.

Stuff the sensible dressing for the weather. This woman wants a power dress.

Chapter 12

The CN Tower really does live up to those visitor guide promises. The view across the city is stunning, and Andy laughs as I gingerly step onto the glass floor at the very top.

'Watch yourself in those heels Debbie' he jokes, as I finally bring myself to peer down the glass to the ground over a thousand feet below. Everything looks so miniscule from way up here, a humbling and disconcerting sight.

It's not the place you want to hang around for long though. A quick peek is more than sufficient.

'Now have you seen enough?' Andy asks, amused at my speedy hop across from the glass floor view point.

'Yes, I'm done here for today' I reply, giving him a warm smile. He returns it with a hug and we set off arm-in-arm to meet Lauren.

Andy has chosen a cosy little French restaurant, just a short drive away from the Tower. Once inside, we could be in Paris, the walls adorned with posters of can-can dancers and the iconic landmarks of that beautiful city. I can't help wondering whether Philippe Roux knows this place?

Lauren isn't due to meet us until 6pm, so we have half an hour to enjoy a drink and a chat. Sticking to his strict rule of never drinking alcohol and driving, Andy orders a cranberry juice while I - despite the early time of day - opt for a Margarita cocktail.

'Well, I am on holiday - sort of' I say, as the cocktail arrives with a ring of salt on the glass rim. Just how I like it.

'You know, mom and dad are really taken with you' Andy says, dipping into the small bowl of mixed nuts the waiter has left for us.

'The feeling is mutual' I reply, feeling ridiculously pleased to have gained their approval.

'You know I can't wait to meet them again' I add, just to reinforce my point. It's not necessary but Andy is clearly delighted.

The conversation quickly turns to Lauren and it's becoming even more obvious just how much Andy loves her.

'The thing is Debbie, I'm thinking of asking her to get engaged.' Andy looks across to see my reaction.

I give him another broad smile, one that reads 'that doesn't surprise me one little bit.' And it doesn't.

'Only thinking about it...?' I reply, giving him a playful push.

He laughs and shrugs his shoulder.

'No, what I mean is that I am going to ask her. On her birthday which is on January 4. We'll be away on a skiing holiday'

'Oh that sounds so romantic Andy. So have you already got a ring?'

He looks thoughtful for a moment, before replying that he hasn't bought it yet but has got his eye on one he knows she'll love. I can see him glancing across at my left hand and I'm still wearing the gold wedding ring David put on my finger all those years ago.

'Do you want to see it?' I say, slipping off the ring. 'It's a Celtic wedding band made from Cornish gold.'

Andy holds it up, reading the tiny inscription on the inside of the band. 'For the love of my life'.

'That's beautiful Debbie, lovely words.'

Again, I smile across and him and nod. But the smile doesn't reach my eyes. If only he could hear what I was thinking.

'Yeh and a fat lot it meant in the long run.' Of course I simply nod in agreement.

'I hope you don't mind me asking this Debbie but do you think you'd ever consider another relationship? I mean you are still quite young...' His voice tails off and I can see is he worried that he might have put his foot in it.

I immediately put him at ease.

'Well, it's funny you should say that. The friend I'm going to New York with - Kevin - wants us to take things further. He's now split from his wife and...'

I'm reluctant to tell Andy that on one occasion I did sleep with Kevin, so I just let the sentence hover for a few seconds.

'And...?' Andy clearly wants to know more.

'And we're thinking about taking our relationship to the next stage. You know, become a couple.' I can feel myself blushing, damn it.

'I hope it works out for you' Andy replies, clocking my reddening face.

'Thanks. We'll take things slowly and see how it goes. He's ten years younger than me...' Again my words tail off and I'm not sure how he'll react to the age difference.

I needn't have worried.

'Good on you Debbie. I don't expect you've said anything yet to your daughter?'

Before I have a chance to reply, I can see Andy's expression change and he waves across the room. Lauren has arrived.

The next few minutes are a blur of introductions and hugs. Lauren is even more stunning in the flesh and is wearing a beautifully cut pale pink trouser suit. It says 'expensive' in an understated sort of way. Her long blonde hair is tied up in a loose bun and I can see that she is already attracting admiring glances from around the room.

'I'll have what Debbie is having' she says, approving of my choice of cocktail.

'Another one for you Debbie?' Andy asks, eyeing my receding glass.

'Why not?' I reply, smiling across at Lauren. She gives a 'thumbs up' gesture and sits down alongside me. She's wearing a floral scent that I recognise from somewhere and a glistening tennis bracelet that I'm pretty sure is a real diamond one.

'That's a gorgeous bracelet' I remark, as the light bounces off the exquisitely cut jewels.

'Isn't it just?' she replies, putting her arm up for me to get a better view. 'It was my first present from Andy, after we'd been together for a year.'

'Well you've got good taste Andy' I reply, holding back on the question I really want to ask. Are those babies for real?

I think I'm a pretty good judge of these things and I bet I'm right. That trinket will have cost a fortune.

It doesn't take long for me to recognise that Lauren is not one for lots of small talk. After a quick run through of my time in Toronto so far, she pushes the conversation straight towards my decision to meet with Andy and his adoptive parents.

'So Debbie - how did you feel when you first heard from Andy?'

I've only just met her and if I'm honest, it all seems a bit too quick. Perhaps it's just her way, straightforward and no nonsense. Or maybe she's just doing her bit to check me out as a way of protecting Andy. Still, we are talking very personal stuff here.

As if sensing my unease, Andy suggests that we get the food order out of the way before settling into our chat.

'The seafood crepes here are amazing' he says, passing over the menu.

Maybe I'm imagining it, but I'm sure I see a flash of irritation move across Lauren's face as Andy interrupts her line of questioning. It doesn't last for long though, and we're soon distracted by orders of delicious sounding food.

Then a big swig of that Margarita.

I can sense Lauren is on a mission to learn as much as she can about me. And she isn't going to hang back.

Yes, Andy's chosen himself a kick-ass kind of girl, an archer with her bow pointed straight ahead.

With yours truly as her target.

Chapter 13

Lauren's questions are coming thick and fast. Some I'm prepared for – 'what was it like when you first saw Andy?' – but there are others that throw me.

'That party you went to must have had...you know some boys that you knew? Did you ever wonder about the father?'

I take another sip of my cocktail, trying not to look as uncomfortable as I feel by Lauren's forensic interview. I deliberately use the word 'interview' because that's exactly what it seems like. Lauren's specialism is psychology and boy don't I know it.

'Well Lauren it was a long time ago and it was a party I just sort of tagged along to. My best friend was there but I didn't really know anyone else. Then I got plied with alcohol and maybe something more... I don't know. All I remember in waking up in a strange bedroom...'

Lauren is staring across at me with a face that is superficially showing pity but the real picture is one of horror. I know what she's thinking. You were raped, sexually abused while under the influence of alcohol and heaven only knows what else.

Not quite right Lauren. Far from it in fact.

'Still we've found each other now and that's all that matters' Andy interrupts, again spotting my discomfiture. He's such a sensitive soul and knows exactly when to come to the rescue. Lauren on the other hand is far from through.

'Yes of course. It's fantastic that you have found each other.' She smiles over at Andy but doesn't make eye contact with me. I think she suspects that I'm not telling the whole truth and being the psychologist that she is, she wants to drill things down.

By the time we've finished the meal, I feel that I've been through the biggest bout of brain boxing that I've ever experienced. I'm mentally and emotionally shattered.

After they've dropped me back at the hotel, I head straight for the shower. I don't really need one but at the same time it's exactly what I want. A sort of cleansing ritual, literally putting some clear water between Lauren and me before meeting up with Philippe Roux.

Earlier this evening, while Lauren had gone off to the 'rest room', Andy leaned across and asked me what I thought of her. Of course I used all the right words – 'beautiful, bright, feisty, refreshingly honest' – but there was another description that I didn't articulate.

Blunt, probing and quite frankly a bit scary.

Andy seemed delighted when I spoke of Lauren

in such glowing terms. After all, if everything goes to plan we'll be related won't we? Hell's bells.

The shower has done its trick and I feel re-energised as I head down to the bar to meet Philippe. He's already there, standing up to greet me as I walk towards him.

'Debbie – so lovely to see you.' We exchange continental style air kisses before setting off on the walk to the little wine bar Philippe has chosen. The outside temperature has already dropped and I'm trying not to shiver in my inappropriately flimsy coat. Mercifully, the place really is a short trot from the hotel, tucked away down a tiny side street.

It's clear that Philippe is a bit of a wine buff and he suggests a bottle of French red which I suspect comes with a hefty price tag. He hasn't eaten yet so orders a selection of small tapas style dishes.

'How did your talk go?' I ask, as he approvingly holds up his wine glass to admire the colour.

'Oh fine. It's all a bit of a treadmill actually – I've given that talk so often that could do it in my sleep. What do you think of the wine then Debbie?'

It's my cue to shut up talking about his work and to get down to appreciating his choice of vino. I have to say it is a great tasting wine, smooth and a nice hint of blackberry.

'This is lovely Philippe. You obviously know your wines.'

He smiles, relishing the compliment.

'My grandfather owned a vineyard in France. When we were children we'd help with the harvest. You could say wine is in my blood.' He laughs throatily, helping himself to a slice of what looks like onion laden pizza bread.

'Pissaladiere French delicacy' he says, asking if I'd like to try a piece.

I decline, explaining that I've just finished off a meal with some 'friends'. Before he can ask any questions about them, I side-track him with my earlier exploration of the Harbourfront area and visit to the CN Tower.

The conversation is light and easy – just what both of us want. Philippe because he's all professionally talked out and me because I've been through the emotional wringer with Lauren. I'm actually enjoying myself and whether it's the wine or the company – probably both – I can feel myself starting to relax.

'You haven't said too much about yourself' Philippe says, after I've quizzed him about his own background. Upper middle class French family who emigrated to Canada in the 1950s; a top university degree followed by veterinary research and frontline practice. A wife who is an infant teacher and they've been married for over 30 years, with three grown up children all of them girls. He's also just become a granddad for the first time and clearly dotes on his little grandson. Philippe has had a blessed life and has the air of a man who is happy in his skin.

'Well you know I have a daughter, Amy, at university, that I lost my husband at an early age and that I work for a magazine' I reply, really wishing that we could just stay on the subject of his life.

'Exactly. Those are the headlines - what I really want to know is more about you. What makes Debbie tick?' He laughs as he takes a slurp of wine, while I can feel myself blushing. I seem to be doing a lot of that these days.

I hardly know where to start but the wine has kicked in nicely and somehow bearing my soul to a stranger seems a perfectly OK thing to do.

We chat about my love of travel, the Cornish coast and countryside, my move from feature writer to organising editorial events, my daughter and my marriage to David before his untimely death at the age of 50.

It's only when we get to this last bit that I can feel my voice start to falter. Philippe looks concerned, offering his apology if he has upset me.

'No not at all' I reply, clearing my throat. 'It's just that I recently discovered something about David and it has shocked me to the core.'

Philippe signals to the waiter that he'd like some more wine and ignores my comment that it's my turn to pay.

Then it all comes tumbling out. How I discovered David's betrayal in a hidden package of birthday and Valentine cards which had been secreted underneath my old garden shed. Cards that told only one story.

That he'd been having an affair with a much younger woman and work colleague called Jemma.

I describe my sense of utter betrayal and the ordeal of going through a second bereavement. How I feel that I've not only lost David but also my conviction that our marriage was rock solid. As solid as the Cornish granite landscape.

Philippe hasn't said much while I've been talking. His eyes are kind though and full of empathy. It's all I want really, just someone to lend a sympathetic ear.

When he does speak, he asks me if I plan to meet up with Jemma.

'I think I have to Philippe. A good friend who has gone through a similar thing, has suggested that I do meet with her.'

Philippe stays silent for a few moments, as if weighing up how to respond.

'I think your friend is right. You need to have that talk, however difficult. I think it will somehow be... what's the word?... empowering.' He reaches over to refill my wine glass and I'm happy to continue drinking. I feel comfortable with Philippe and the fact that I hardly know him still doesn't seem to matter.

'Now this friend of yours you are talking about. It's not this 'Charlie' one you've been visiting?'

'No not Charlie. It's someone else, my very first boyfriend actually...'

'Oh...' Philippe is clearly interested in hearing more.

And to hell with it. I'm all tired out with lying.

Philippe is about to become the second person to hear about 'Mr DJ'.

Question is, how much more do I dare to bare my soul?

Chapter 14

Keeping things simple, I tell Philippe about venturing up into my old house loft to clear things out before the house move.

I describe finding my old teenage diary, stirring up memories of my first proper boyfriend, a nightclub disc jockey known locally as 'Mr DJ'. I also tell him how I lied about my age back then, pretending that I was 19 and working in the fashion industry.

'The thing is Philippe, I was only a few weeks away from my 16th birthday but I looked a lot older when I was dressed up to the nines.'

I'm looking for signs of disapproval, a frown that says 'tut tut' but there is no such thing. Philippe just maintains an air of interested neutrality, the sort of face that could belong to a diplomat.

'Anyway, I decided to write to him - a good old-fashioned handwritten letter - and he replied.' Philippe nods, wanting me to continue.

I fill him in with details about Mr DJ. His big English country house in Buckinghamshire, his failed marriages and children, his old juke box collection, a second home in Tenerife and the fact that I'd found out he'd been lying about his age all those years ago as well. Instead of the mid-twenties Mr DJ I thought I'd been dating, he was then a decade older.

'Oh' Philippe responds, taking a sip of his wine. 'That's quite an age gap.'

It's simply an observation with no hint of judgement involved. I like him for that.

'Yes I suppose so but...' I don't have time to reply before I'm interrupted by my mobile phone ringing out. I recognise that it's Ashley's number which means that Amy is taking advantage of her boyfriend's phone largesse - yet again.

'Is it all right if I take this Philippe?' I ask, adding apologetically that 'I won't be long'.

'No problem' he replies, shrugging good humouredly.

'Hang on I need to step outside' I tell Amy, and already I've picked up that there's something wrong. It's there in the tone of her voice, a sense of urgency and concern.

'Mum, now you mustn't panic. I wanted to tell you straight away but everything is OK really. It's just that... Kevin's been in an accident.'

I only register the words 'Kevin' and 'accident' and suddenly I feel sick. The combination of too much wine, the sudden blast of cold air and Amy's strained voice.

'Mum... are you alright..?'

I take a few deep breaths and steady myself against the freezing outside wall.

'What's happened Amy? I need to know exactly...is Kevin hurt?'

'He's broken his ankle in two places mum. He came off his new bike on his way into work. He's at the hospital now and asked me to ring you. He's fine but he won't be travelling to New York...' Her voice tails off as I frantically take in the information.

'What's this about a bike?' I ask, still leaning hard against the wall. My heart rate has gone into overdrive and I'm desperately trying not to hyper-ventilate.

'He got himself a new scooter apparently. He was turning into work when he hit a bit of ice and went sideways. At least he was going slowly, so it could have been a lot worse.' I can hear already that Amy has calmed down - probably a counter reaction to my own state of shock.

Assured now that Kevin is as well as can be expected, and that as we speak is being looked after at the hospital, my brain goes into practical mode. We've got a hotel and flights booked for New York in a few days time which I'll need to cancel. And I have to speak to Kevin as soon as possible, whatever time that turns out to be over here.

'Mum, Ashley has had an idea. Why don't we join you in New York? Ashley is happy to pay and I've got my savings as well...'

Her suggestion throws me, as I've already made

up my mind to cancel everything and get the earliest flight home.

'Mum... did you hear...?'

'Yes' I reply, more testily than intended. 'Look darling I just want to get home, Kevin will need help until he's mobile again. There's no way I'm going to New York now.'

Amy doesn't respond and I can sense her disappointment. I'm also miffed at Ashley for putting the idea in her head.

'Let's at least sleep on it mum. You've had a nasty shock.' Yet again Amy taking on the parent role, a thing she developed after David died.

'All right I won't do anything until I've spoken to Kevin' I say, suddenly aware just how cold I've got in the few minutes I've been on the phone.

'Where are you mum? Are you with someone?' Amy acting the surrogate parent again. Bless her.

'Yes, I'm with a friend of... erm... Charlie's' I reply, a bit too quickly. 'I'll head straight back to the hotel now and wait for Kevin to call.'

'Promise you won't be up all night worrying mum? Kevin really is fine, it's just the ankle and a few cuts and bruises.'

As if that isn't enough. Why did he go and buy himself a stupid scooter anyway?

By the time I get back inside the wine bar, I'm shivering uncontrollably and straight away Philippe picks up that something is wrong.

'Listen Philippe - I need to get back to the hotel. I'll tell you all about it on the way.'

And with that we are off into the bitterly cold night, Philippe insisting that I put on his overcoat for the short walk back.

It suddenly occurs to me that he never did get to hear the full Mr DJ story.

Perhaps things, even bad ones, really do happen for a reason.

Meantime, I need to get hold of that other significant man in my life - Andy. Our carefully thought-out visitor itinerary is about to be shattered.

A bit like poor Kevin's ankle.

Chapter 15

On the way back, I fill Philippe in with the news. He's sympathetic and offers to buy me a nightcap - 'a brandy will help with the shock' - but I politely decline. It might well help with shock but not with the brain power and right now I need my wits about me.

He gives me his mobile phone number so I can call him if I need any more help.

'What return flight are you going for?' he asks when we get to the hotel reception.

'Oh, I'll get the earliest one available. It might be tomorrow but more likely the day after. I'll let you know.'

'Debbie I hope this isn't the last time I'll see you before you head back. But if it turns out that way, then it's been a real pleasure to meet you.' His face tells me that he means it and we exchange another continental style kiss on each cheek followed by a brief hug.

It's rare that I feel so comfortable with a new acquaintance and I do hope that I'll get to see Philippe again. If not on this visit, then perhaps on my return. And under the circumstances, I think that a second trip is a given.

Once alone, I put in a call to Andy and explain what has happened. He immediately goes into his soothing doctor mode.

'Don't worry - I'll sort everything out with mom and dad. Just let me know when you have rearranged your flight and we'll take things from there.'

'I'm so sorry that I might have to cut things short Andy. Hopefully we'll have another full day before I fly back. It would be lovely to see Theresa and Joe again...'

'I'm sure we'll work out a way of us all getting together before you head off' he replies, just as I realise that I haven't mentioned Lauren.

'And Lauren too..' I add, hoping he hasn't noticed the omission.

'Hmm that might be tricky. She's off on a training course tomorrow morning for three days.'

Funny, I don't recall her mentioning that earlier but then why would she? It might explain way she seemed a bit tense, especially if she had things to do before setting off. Come to think of it, I can hear a female voice singing in the background and I suspect it is Lauren. Hopefully I haven't interrupted their romantic evening together.

'Do give her my best wishes' I add, and he promises to do so. If it is Lauren I can hear in the distance, Andy isn't asking her to come to the phone.

It seems an age before I get the call from Kevin and he's still at the hospital.

'Bloody hell, are you OK?' I ask, wondering if the delay might mean that he's got concussion as well.

'Honestly Debbie, I'm fine - apart from this damn broken ankle. I'm waiting for the X-rays to come back and then they'll slap on a temporary plaster cast. I just want out of here now.'

I then get the full story about what happened. On a whim, he decided to buy himself a motor scooter after hearing that a neighbour was selling one off cheaply. Having passed his motorbike test a few years ago, he thought a small scooter would be 'a doddle.' As Amy had said earlier, he was about to turn into the 'Cornwall Now' car park when he lost control of the bike.

'That was it Debbie. Next thing I know I'm on my side, my right ankle caught under the damn scooter. Felt like a right prat.' He laughs, but it's more of a reaction to feeling stupid rather than amusement.

'I'm going to get an early flight back' I say, adding that I've already identified one which leaves the day after tomorrow.

'There's no need. I'll be fine and Ginny has offered to help out here until I can get myself up and about again.'

Ginny. His estranged wife. I wasn't expecting that one.

'Ginny...?' I can't bring myself to finish the sentence.

'I know. But we've been getting on a lot better now the divorce is pretty much settled. And it will be nice to have the kids around for a bit more.'

We're interrupted by a nurse telling Kevin that his X-ray results are on their way.

It gives me a breathing space to take in the Ginny situation.

When he gets back on the phone, I tell him that I'll stay in Toronto until the end of the week as planned but that I won't be going on to New York.

'Look why don't you let Amy have my ticket? You two could have a lovely girly Christmas shopping trip' he suggests. I know he's only trying to make a good situation out of a bad one, but the whole point of the New York trip was for us to spend some quality time together and decide on our future.

'Actually Amy has already asked me if she can fly out with Ashley' I reply, hoping that he doesn't hear the disappointment in my voice. Disappointment that he doesn't seem to need me back home as soon as possible.

Disappointment that his soon to be 'former' wife will be looking after him instead of me.

And disappointment that we won't be able to discuss our future relationship in an exciting place miles away from home.

Our conversation is brought to a halt when Kevin's X-ray results are delivered. It's a double 'tib and fib' break and he'll be laid up for a few weeks before he's allowed to put any weight on the ankle.

So that's it then. I won't cut short the Toronto trip but I need to decide what to do about our New York plane tickets. It seems churlish not to let Amy and Ashley have the chance of a weekend in New York, but I'd really like to meet the boyfriend properly before he sets off on a jaunt to the Big Apple with my daughter.

As Amy suggested, I'll sleep on it. That's if I can manage any shut-eye given the past few hours.

The Ginny situation is still bugging me. I know that people can remain friends after they have split up and it's only right that they do for the sake of their two boys.

But what if adversity brings them closer - close enough to call off their impending divorce? I know I'm being ridiculous and that things have probably gone way too far for that to happen.

And that's the point. It is the little word 'probably' that is bothering me. I'd prefer 'definitely' to be used instead, but I'm not writing a feature piece now. This is real life, messy and complicated.

Just a few months ago, before they split up, things were pretty simple. Kevin was my best friend and soul mate. It was safe, asexual ground, where he was spoken for and I had no desire to go into another relationship.

Easy peasy, lemon squeezy.

But that was before his estrangement from Ginny and before we slept together.

Before Kevin asked me if I thought we could become a couple.

Before I confided in Kevin about the child I had given up for adoption nearly four decades ago.

Above all, it was before I discovered that my late husband had been screwing someone behind my back.

You see I've already made up my mind that yes, I really do want to be part of a couple again. To share my life with my best and most trusted friend.

New York was going to be the place where I told Kevin this, a place that would always be special for us.

'New York, New York' as the song goes.

Instead, it's a return to Truro with the prospect that we might not even get to that stage.

Damn it Kevin, why did you buy that cheap scooter? A life path possibly cut off for something so trivial.

Suddenly, the prospect of that brandy Philippe was offering seems tempting.

It's gone 12pm but something tells me that Monsieur Roux, like me, will still be wide awake.

Chapter 16

There is no answer from Philippe's room, so he's either in a deep sleep or he's not around. I could try his mobile but that feels a bit intrusive at this hour.

Calling room service for a large brandy just seems sad, so I'll just have to settle for sachet of hotel instant coffee. Hardly the thing to help with getting to sleep but a better option than the insipid tea bags.

At some point I must have dozed off because I'm woken abruptly by the sound of a trolley being trundled along the corridor and muffled voices outside. A quick glance at my watch shows it is 7.30am - far too early to get up really but what the heck.

I'd better give my lovely son another ring before he heads off to work - assuming he hasn't done so already. When Andy eventually answers, I can hear traffic sounds in the background and recall that he'd said something last night about dropping Lauren off at the rail station.

'It's OK Debbie, Lauren's already on the train' he says, after I apologise for having a 'senior moment'.

He is delighted when I give him the news that I'll be staying on for another few days as planned. So the trip to Niagara Falls with Theresa and Joe can go ahead, along with their plan for a dinner at their house afterwards.

'That's great Debbie. Mom and dad will be so pleased'.

Back to square one then. Theresa and Joe are due to pick me up this morning and Andy will join us later. While I'm excited about accompanying them to Niagara Falls, I hope that being in their company will feel as easy as it did the first time.

In the event, everything is hunky dory. Theresa and Joe are excellent companions, showing me the sights as only locals can. The falls are humbling and awe inspiring, while the drive into the surrounding countryside takes my breath away. And surprisingly perhaps, not a word is said about the deeper things we spoke about just a couple of nights ago.

'Now Debbie - why don't you stay over at our place tonight? We've got a room all made up and we can drop you back at the hotel tomorrow morning.' Theresa smiles across in a way that makes it hard to turn down her invitation.

We're sitting in a cosy cafe with steaming mugs of hot chocolate - just the thing needed after our long walk.

'That's really sweet of you' I reply, my hands wrapped around the mug for warmth. 'I'll need to go back to grab a change of clothes though.'

So that's settled then. A stay over at chez Theresa and Joe's and sleeping in Andy's old childhood bedroom. If you'd told me this just a few months ago, I'd have scoffed in disbelief. And even now I'm mentally pinching myself, still barely able to believe that I'm actually here. As I've said before, it's like playing a role in someone else's surreal movie. Lights, camera, action.

Theresa and Joe's house is an older three storey town property in a pretty tree lined street. It's what I call a 'Tardis' type house, like the one in my favourite childhood TV programme. While the outside looks narrow and compact, the inside is enormous with an entrance hall bigger than the whole of my little place back home.

All the rooms are cavernous with high ceilings and huge windows. The furnishings are old style to reflect the age of the house, with impressive wall to ceiling bookshelves in the main family room. The term 'shabby chic' comes to mind - comfortable and definitely lived in. The pole opposite of Andy's trendy minimalist apartment.

We're standing in the kitchen, with its Shaker style units and range cooker. Theresa has pre-prepared a casserole which smells divine and I've joined her to put together a starter of smoked fish and salad.

'So this friend of yours, Kevin, is all right apart from the broken ankle?' Theresa asks, chopping into some plump tomatoes that look like they've been on steroids.

'Yes, but it's a bad break. He won't be able to get around properly for some time.'

Theresa hands me a pile of cut tomatoes to add to the salad bowl. I can guess what she's thinking - how come you need to get back so quickly to look after a mere 'friend'.

'Actually Theresa, he's a bit more than a pal. We go back a long way and we've come a lot closer recently....'

She stops chopping and glances across at me, a knowing smile on her face.

'Hey Debbie - I thought as much. When you said you were vacationing in New York, I figured that there might be a bit more to it.'

I can feel myself blush again and imagine my face colour blending in with the pile of tomatoes I'm looming over.

'Yes, well we were supposed to be taking time in New York to discuss our future - you know, whether we should become a proper couple and maybe move in together.'

I'm hoping Theresa hasn't noticed my flushed appearance as I busy myself with salad arranging.

'That's good Debbie' she replies, this time handing me a pile of sliced spring onions - or 'scallions' as she calls them.

There's an awkward silence as she waits for me to continue the conversation. Should I mention that his former wife is moving back in to look after him, for goodness knows how long?

Hmm, better not..

'Still Theresa it could be a lot worse' I say eventually, just to fill the gap. She nods, adding that Andy has had his fair share of grim road accidents to deal with over the years.

'And I suppose Kevin doesn't know anything about Andy - or us?' she then asks, looking up again to see my reaction.

It's a fair enough question, especially as she is already aware that I haven't told another member of my family, not even my late husband.'

'Actually yes, he does' I reply, clocking the flicker of surprise on her face. 'I just had to confide in someone and Kevin is my closest friend.'

We don't have time to continue the conversation before Andy arrives carrying the biggest portion of smoked salmon that I've ever laid my eyes on.

'Main course delivered as instructed' he announces handing it across to Theresa.

'Hope you've got a big appetite!.'

Joseph then appears with a bottle of champagne and four flute glasses. He doesn't waste any time in opening it and laughs as the cork comes out with an almighty bang, almost hitting the ceiling light.

'To us and the future whatever it holds' he says, raising his glass.

As our glasses clink together in a toast, I realise that despite Kevin's accident, I feel happier than I have done for a long time.

'To us and the future' I say, echoing Joseph's words while deliberately omitting the last bit - 'whatever it holds'.

Somehow those last three words sound sinister and tonight should all about basking in the glow of new friendship and family.

Yes, because family they are now and will be for the rest of my days.

Theresa then raises her glass and proposes another toast.

'To Debbie - thank you for coming into our lives'.

As our glasses clink together again, I have tears in my eyes.

Tears of relief and joy.

Chapter 17

In the film that seems to be my life at the moment, I'll just press the fast forward button.

Now I'm back home in Truro and that thing they call 'jet lag' has definitely kicked in - why does it always seem worse on the way home from long haul travel? It barely seems possible that less than 24 hours ago I was still thousands of miles across the Atlantic.

Only the night before last, I was sleeping in Andy's old boyhood bedroom, complete with posters of his sporting heroes, music idols, (it seems that he was into grunge bands like Nirvana), and vintage racing cars.

I'm sure it wasn't as neat and tidy when he was there for real and it was easy to imagine him squatting over the small desk in the corner as he revised for his exams. In the far corner there was a shelf groaning with sporting trophies - basketball and swimming were the main ones - and dotted around were photos of school friends, all looking exuberant with their whole lives ahead of them.

Being in the younger Andy's room reminded me how much I missed Amy and now that I'm home I can't wait to see her. She'll be back from university in a few hours time and tomorrow her boyfriend Ashley is joining us. Finally, I'll get to meet him and not before time.

Meantime, I've got a few hours to unpack and have a quick bath before Kevin gets here. He'll be coming by taxi and will need help getting in and out of his wheelchair on my unfriendly drive way.

Of course I'm excited about seeing him and just hope that I don't look as wiped out as I feel. I've bought him a jokey present of a bandaged teddy bear sitting astride a motorbike - a bit sick I know, given he's just had an accident on one, but I think he'll see the funny side.

As things turned out, my final few days in Canada disappeared in a blur and before I knew it I was at the airport, saying tearful goodbyes to Andy, Theresa and Joe. No Lauren because she was on her course but she did ring the night before wishing me a good journey back. Truth is, I still don't know what to make of her and I suspect she feels the same way about me.

'Whatever you decide about the future, do stay in touch' Theresa told me as I prepared to make my way towards the departure gate.

'Absolutely I will' I replied, my voice cracking. Joe and Andy were trying to appear upbeat, smiling and waving as I made my way across to the gate. Theresa just looked preoccupied, keeping whatever thoughts she was having to herself.

Instinctively I rushed back over to give them all

one last hug. Taken by surprise, Andy held me tightly while Theresa and Joe joined in what can only be described as a family group hug. By now all of us were fighting back the tears and none of us wanted to be the first to let go.

Then the last clipped flight announcement, for travellers heading to London.

'Give me a call when you land' Andy shouted across as I finally ran back towards the departure gate.

I blew a kiss and waved, aware that my eye make-up must be running down my face in grotesque rivulets. The flight check-in attendant looked sympathetic and smiled as if to say 'yes these goodbyes suck don't they?'

I returned her smile just to be polite but didn't say anything. I just wanted to board the plane and try to sleep. And against the odds I managed it, wearing an eye mask and a naff looking sign saying 'do not disturb'.

Next thing I knew we were landing at Heathrow and after quick calls to Andy, Kevin and Amy, I made my way across to Paddington station for the long train journey back to Cornwall. This time I didn't sleep but pretended to read a newspaper and flicked distractedly through a glossy society magazine. In reality, I was reliving every second of my Canadian visit including my confessional drink with Monsieur Roux.

I never did get to see Philippe again before I left

but I've already decided to stay in touch. Sometimes complete strangers leave a mark on your life, a feeling that you have met them for a reason. That's certainly true of him and I knew it from the first time our paths crossed in that cramped hotel bar. Was it really only a week ago?

I've just stepped out of the bath when my phone rings out and it's Kevin telling me that his taxi is due any time.

'Now just to warn you - I've got a few cuts and bruises on my face. I'll need you to push the wheelchair over your front door step - think you're up to it?'

I laugh saying that my suitcase probably weighs more than him, wheelchair and all.

'If I can navigate Heathrow with a case on wheels, your chair will be fine' I reply, hoping that I'm right.

You only start to notice uneven surfaces and the height of steps when you have a problem to contend with and like it or not, Kevin's broken ankle is a challenge.

The Edwardian architects who designed my house didn't think about disability access or even prams for that matter. For them high steps looked the part and that was all that mattered. Design over functionality.

I'm on my second cup of strong coffee when I hear the taxi pulling up on the driveway. Here we go, let's see how we can manoeuvre the wheelchair over these damned steps.

I try not to look shocked when I see Kevin but fail abysmally. A few cuts and bruises? His face is swollen on one side, with a deep still raw looking gash across his chin. Both eyes are bruised, the left one so badly that it looks a bit like an eye patch. He has a large shiny plastic knee high cover over his right leg and it takes several minutes to get him out of the taxi.

We both exchange awkward smiles, not quite knowing what to say.

'A bit battered you said...?' I gingerly touch the side of his face, not feeling brave enough to plant a kiss. The jovial taxi driver is lifting the wheelchair out of the boot, whistling as he deftly pushes it into position.

'Do you want some help in getting this inside?' he asks, trundling it over the unevenly paved driveway.

'Oh that would be great' I reply, grabbing Kevin's arm and helping him into the chair. He's not a large man but it's surprising how heavy he feels right now and I'm pleased that the taxi driver has offered to lend a hand.

'See you later then - call me when you're ready to go' he says to Kevin, once we've hoisted the wheelchair across the threshold.

Kevin suddenly looks sheepish, mumbling something along the lines of 'OK thanks' and handing a £10 note to the driver.

So he's planning to go home tonight then. I suppose I shouldn't be surprised in the circumstances. After all, it's my first night home and Amy's due later.

But I am taken aback and not exactly in a nice way.

Let's face it. Kevin will be heading back home with Ginny and the boys waiting for him.

And that's exactly my problem.

Chapter 18

The sofa is wedged into the far corner to accommodate Kevin's wheelchair and now my little sitting room seems even pokier than it did before.

'Come on give us a proper kiss then' Kevin quips, wincing as he pushes out his bruised lips in my direction.

I give him perfunctory peck and flinch at the sight of his battered face close up.

'I know, I look a bloody mess but hey - it's great to see you back' he says, giving me a crooked smile. Poor Kevin, he must be in considerable pain but is still managing to keep upbeat.

'I don't suppose you're allowed to drink beer or wine in your state?' I reply, still trying to hide my irritation that he's heading back home tonight.

'Stuff that, I could murder a beer - come on, you know me better than that Debbie.'

I should have guessed that Kevin would take zero notice of any sensible advice given by his doctor, whether he's on pain killers or not.

'Well I shouldn't encourage you but I'll let you have a glass - and just the one mind.'

Then the sudden realisation that I'm starting to sound like his mother. Damn it.

'We'll see about that' he replies, grimacing like a naughty school boy.

Two beers later and we're both beginning to feel more chilled. We're all talked out about Canada - though haven't yet mentioned my meeting with Philippe Roux - and Kevin laughs out loud when I present him with his tubby Canadian toy bear perched on a yellow plastic motor bike.

'Jeez that must have taken some finding – it's genius!' he says, holding up the toy and prodding the ridiculous pot belly.

'Not really - I spotted it in a toy shop, it's a bit sick I know...'

'No I love it and his bike is in a lot better state than my one. Mine's a write off.'

'Well at least it's only the bike that's written off' I say, squeezing Kevin's hand. This time we kiss more passionately but I can still feel myself holding back. Kevin senses something is wrong and gives me one of his knowing sideways looks.

'Are you all right Debbie? You just seem - I don't know - a bit preoccupied...?' It's observation as well as a question but he does have a point.

'Not really - just travel-weary I suppose.' I'm bluffing and he knows it.

'Come on, spill. There's more to it than that.' As usual Kevin isn't going to be fobbed off and I should know by now that I can't hide anything from him.

'Well...I suppose I'm just a bit disappointed that you aren't staying over tonight.' There I've said it.

For once Kevin is taken aback, a flicker of surprise crossing his battered face.

'Oh Debbie - I just thought I was doing the right thing. What with Amy due back and me being in this state...'

He takes hold of my hand and suddenly I feel stupid for thinking that his motives are driven by anything other than a genuine concern for me.

'Hang on...you're not worried about me being back at home with Ginny are you?'

I know that my face says it all. Yes I bloody well am.

'Debbie, come on. You know the score with Ginny and nothing has changed. She's just been helping me out and we're trying to keep things good between us for the boys' sake.'

Then it all comes tumbling out. How bitterly upset I am about us not being able to go to New York, how I wanted us to talk about our future in a place well away from home and how jealous - yes jealous - I am that it is Ginny looking after him and not me.

There you go. Me being selfish, insecure and needy. Not a description I'm proud of.

'Look, first of all you've got no reason to be

jealous of Ginny - she won't even be my wife in a month's time.' He pauses to look me full in the eyes to reinforce his point.

'And second - if you want I can ring right now and tell her that I've changed my mind. That I'm stopping over at yours tonight.'

He's trying to make me feel better but now I just feel like a selfish prick, ridiculous and clingy.

'No, don't do that Kevin - sorry it's just me being silly.'

I know exactly what has caused this and it's the shock discovery of David's betrayal. That coupled with the emotional roller coaster of finally meeting up with my adopted son and his family.

And as if all of this wasn't enough, there's Kevin's accident and temporary physical confinement.

Let's face it, who wouldn't be sideswiped by this combination?

When I relay all this to Kevin, he's sympathetic, adding that he feels guilty for piling on even more pressure. God, we could both go around in circles like this.

We leave it that he'll head home tonight but will move into my place sooner rather than later. Besides, I'll need a bit of time to get the place ready and to free up more space

'Now promise you won't be fretting any more about me and Ginny' Kevin says as we wait by the front door for his taxi.

Between us we've managed to steer his wheelchair back outside and he even managed to get himself to the loo and back in one piece. Small victories over adversity.

'Promise I won't' I reply, giving him a long hug. He looks so vulnerable and again I mentally kick myself for any stupid doubts I've had about his relationship with his soon to be 'former' wife.

Alone again, I've got few more hours to rest before Amy gets here.

Well I think I have - until the doorbell rings out.

When I answer it, old Ted my next door neighbour, is standing there wearing that heavy brown overcoat that seems welded to his back.

'Welcome home Debbie' he says, his crinkly face breaking into a grin. 'So how was your holiday?'

'Ah Ted - nice to see you again too.' Inwardly I'm cursing of course.

He's hovering by the door waiting to be let in but no way is that going to happen.

'Listen Ted, Amy's due home and I've got a bath running. Could I pop around tomorrow and tell you all about Canada?'

'Tomorrow - um I've got one of my lady friends calling around in the afternoon. I could do the morning though.'

Desperate to get rid of him, I arrange to see him

for a coffee at 10am tomorrow.

'Oh by the way Debbie, this came for you when you were away. The postie asked if I'd sign for it.'

He digs a jiffy bag out from his coat pocket and I immediately recognise the writing on the front.

It's from Peter, aka Mr DJ.

And from the feel of things, there is more than just another letter inside.

Chapter 19

Though I'm sorely tempted to rip open the package from Mr DJ, I force myself not to look. Amy will be home soon and the last thing I need is another big distraction.

So I push it to the back of my desk, hidden behind a pile of 'Cornwall Now' magazines and busy myself with tidying up Amy's bedroom. Not that there's much to do as she's left things pretty much as they were. It's clear that she's changed the bedding and I mentally try to get rid of the image of her lying there with Ashley.

Talking of the trust fund boyfriend, I notice that a framed picture of them both has been placed on the dressing table. I can see St Michael's Mount in the background, so I guess it was taken recently on Marazion beach. They both look windswept and carefree, as they should do at their time of life. The look of love though? Frankly it's hard to tell and I'll make up my mind on that one when I see them together.

I've decided to go for the easy option of a pizza delivery tonight. Normally I'm not one for ordering takeout food but there's no way I'm cooking after a long haul journey. Someone once said that life is too short to stuff a mushroom. Well sometimes it's too short to fill your face with home-cooked food and tonight is one of these occasions.

I'm still lingering in Amy's bedroom when I hear her key turning in the front door.

'Hey mum' she shouts out, as I make a sharp exit from her room. I'm so pleased to see her that I nearly lose my footing on the stairs, just about managing to grab hold of the hand rail.

Amy laughs at the surprised expression on my face, before we hug each other and dissolve into a fit of giggles.

'It's bad enough with Kevin hobbling around without you breaking a leg too' Amy jokes, before asking how much duty-free booze I got through on the plane.

'None you cheeky madam and if you must know I slept through the whole of the flight.' Amy gives me one of her sceptical 'oh yeh?' looks before we head to the kitchen for coffee with her demanding to see my holiday photos. Hell's bells, here we go.

'What you lost your camera... mum what are you like?' She's staring in disbelief after I've just told her that there are no photos to show.

'Tell you what mum. I'll put out a call on Facebook to see if anyone has picked up the camera. You get that all the time on there - people who have left their camera somewhere and then the finder publishes a photo asking if anyone recognises the people...'

I'm going to have to get my thinking cap on and damn well quickly.

'Hmm - that won't work. I dropped it in the water when I went out on the boat trip.'

'But mum - Charlie must have taken some pictures too. Can't you get her to just like... email them across?

Good job I'd planned ahead for this one.

'Yes she's going to send some in a few weeks time when she gets back from her mountain retreat...' I'm distracting myself by pouring more coffee so that Amy can't see my face.

'Retreat? What's all that about then....?'

So out I come with the made up story about my old friend Charlie heading off to a retreat in Mexico to help her get over her marriage break up. Amy looks sceptical and I can't say I blame her.

'Sounds like she's a bit weird, like an old hippy. I thought you said she hated hippies when you were growing up?'

'Well people change. Anyway, I'm starving. Shall we order a pizza before I tell you all about it?'

An obvious distraction technique but it works and for now Charlie is forgotten about as we decide on toppings and side orders. Amy is still going through her vegetarian phase despite Ashley's fondness for burgers and all things meaty. So vegi option it is even though I could murder a pepperoni supreme.

While we're waiting for the pizza delivery, I fill Amy in with my trips to Niagara, the CN Tower and explorations of Toronto. She's interested but keeps steering the conversation back to Charlie and her family.

'I spoke to nan the other day and she says she remembers Charlie.' Another of Amy's attempts to get the subject back to my one time best mate.

Before flying out to Canada, I told my sister Carol about the supposed plan to meet with Charlie in Toronto but she only had a fleeting recollection of my teenage friend. Mum was asleep when I rang, so I left it to Carol to tell her where I was heading.

I'm still digesting what Amy has just said about her nan remembering Charlie, when she delivers the next killer line.

'She said Charlie was a cheeky little minx who was always getting you into loads of trouble.'

I laugh nervously, scared that this could get even more complicated. What if my mum has somehow kept in touch with some of Charlie's family? I know they moved away to Scotland in the mid -970s and that there was no love lost between our two households. Certainly, nothing was ever mentioned of Charlie or her family when I made one of my rare trips back to the Midlands.

After my dad died in 1983, mum moved to Wales with Carol and her husband, remaining there ever since. With no children on the scene, there is plenty of room and although quite frail, mum is still able to help with cooking and household chores. It's an arrangement that seems to suit them all.

Still, I hadn't even thought if mum might somehow have an ongoing link to Charlie's family.

'Mum – did you hear what I just said? You seem miles away.'

'Sorry Amy. I was just thinking about Charlie when we were growing up. Yes, she was a bit cheeky back then but your nan would never recognise her now...'

'You'll have to show nan and aunty Carol some photos. How long did you say Charlie was staying at this, er, retreat thingy...?'

Saved by a delivery man, thank the Lord. The question has just popped out of Amy's mouth when the pizzas arrive.

'I'll get it' I say, leaping up from the chair. Small mercies.

I leave Amy to sort things out while I grab a bottle of wine. I swore I wouldn't drink anymore tonight but boy do I really need that glass of vino.

The words by Sir Walter Scott, 'Oh, what a tangled web we weave, when first we practice to deceive!' are going around and around in my head, stuck in a manic loop.

'Mum....?'

Amy is shouting out from the sitting room.

'They've left out the sides of garlic bread and

potato wedges. Shall I give them a call?'

'Go on then – but give me the pizzas to put in the oven.'

I leave Amy to make her protest call, while I help myself to a large slurp of wine.

'Oh, what a tangled – yes, bloody tangled – web we weave.'

You got it right there, Walter. Spot on.

Chapter 20

Well we manage to get through the evening without my Charlie story falling apart. After a while Amy gets bored with hearing about Canada and is happy to switch the conversation to the subject of her and Ashley.

Yes, it seems, he is definitely real boyfriend material and not just a good pal with benefits. And yes, Ashley's a rich boy but has a good social conscience – 'he gives loads to charity and does voluntary work for a homeless group' – Amy tells me, her face lighting up with pride.

I avoid asking her about the 'L' word, not wanting to dig too deeply at this stage. If they do love each other it will show when I see them together.

'You don't mind me and Ashley sleeping together here tomorrow do you?' Amy asks out of the blue.

'Of course not' I reply, trying to sound nonchalant and relaxed, while inwardly feeling just plain awkward.

'You'll like him mum – he's great company.'

And with that she disappears into her bedroom

with me suddenly realising that my little girl really is all grown up.

Too tired to look at whatever Mr DJ has sent to me, I pretty much fall unconscious when I hit the pillow.

But this doesn't last for long and now it's only 6am but I'm wide awake. However much I try to tell myself that mum's distant recollection of Charlie isn't likely to come back to haunt me, something keeps telling me that it might.

Best then to give up on the sleep and head downstairs as quietly as I can. It suddenly hits me that we're only a few weeks away from Christmas, but I haven't given it much thought. This will be the first in my new home and I did manage to bag a few baubles and decorations in Canada.

Over the years, we've stuck to the mound of decorations that David and I collected throughout our married life. Each of them holds memories and as Amy never ceases to recall, her dad was just like a big kid at Christmas.

But this year is all about change and David's affair has left me questioning huge parts of our married life. Like the time he went off on a three day visit to Frankfurt just before what was to be his very last Christmas.

I love German Christmas fairs and asked if I could tag along as well. His curt response took me aback – no, it was a purely work visit and there would be little time for shopping at markets.

'But I wouldn't mind strolling around on my own..' I protested, stung by his terse response. Looking back, he didn't sound like the David I knew and loved.

'Forget it Debbie – no-one else is taking their wives or family. This is a big deal for us and we have to stay focussed.'

I knew there was no point in pursuing it, so reluctantly accepted the situation and put his tetchiness down to stress at work.

Now I know why he didn't want me to go. Jemma, the twenty something colleague he was screwing behind my back was also on that trip. No wonder he bought me back a beautiful exquisitely designed gold necklace. Guilty bloody conscience, that's why.

Needing to distract myself from thoughts of Jezebel Jemma, I check my emails and there's a lovely one from Andy.

'Missing you already Debbie and I hope you have recovered from the journey. Give me a call when you are settled back and mom and dad send their love. Andy xx.'

Immediately I feel cheered up and wing off a reply saying that I'll call him over the weekend when Amy and Ashley have gone back to university.

'Give my love to Lauren as well' I add, suddenly realising that he hadn't mentioned her in his email. Strange that.

Now seems the right time to open Mr DJ's parcel and I'd better make sure that the office door is locked before I examine the contents. There's a short note inside attached to a stash of photographs and a photocopy of a faded 1975 poster from the 'Long Room' nightclub in Birmingham, the place where Mr DJ held court at his popular weekend discos.

Seeing the poster takes me right back to that heady mid-1970s summer when I became the much envied girlfriend of Mr DJ, a bit of a celebrity in his own town. Or so we thought back then.

I'm not prepared for the photos and can feel my heart thumping. There's one of me on the night I was picked out from the crowd by Mr DJ, staying by his side for the rest of the evening.

The smiling 'coming up to her 16th birthday' me, looking much older and leggy in my purple mini skirt and matching wedge shoes.

Mr DJ at his music desk, waving out to someone in the crowd and me again, standing alongside him looking like the proverbial cat that got the cream.

And then, peering out from the crowd, Charlie looking a bit sullen and preoccupied.

There are another two photos of me looking shyly at the camera and perched on a scruffy sofa at Mr DJ's flat. I guess this was taken on one of the first occasions I went to his place, a modern block just across the road from the Edgbaston cricket ground.

Finally, another picture of Mr DJ, standing outside the 'Long Room' club, his scruffy white van clearly visible in the background. He's wearing some hideous velvet trousers and a garishly patterned shirt, opened at the front with a huge collar. The fashion may be awful but his handsome rakish smile, the one that I fell for all those years ago, is there frozen in time.

I'm so absorbed with the pictures that I haven't even read the note yet. I can see that he's written it in haste, as his usually neat writing is a bit more loose and raggedy around the edges.

'Hi Debbie,

I meant to put these with my last letter and then realised I'd forgotten. (What do they say about getting older?!). Found these when I was going through some old stuff and thought you'd like to see them. They are copies so you can keep them. You were saying how few pictures you had from back then and I'd no idea that I still had these until I discovered them tucked behind some LPs – remember those?! You look so young and beautiful – just as I remember. There you go – it proves that 'secret' I mentioned about having real feelings for you, the thing that frightened me off. Anyway enjoy and isn't that your mate Charlie hovering in the background? What about that poster? I bet it will bring back the memories like it did for me. As for my outfit, well sorry is all I can say – what the hell was I thinking about?! Look forward to your next letter......Peter x '

I re-read the note several times, pausing over the line about his previously secret feelings for me. The pictures are strewn around, still frames of memories and another world.

And there is Charlie, staring out at me with an expression that I remember from old. She wore that stroppy pout a lot and that night she was worried about what would happen to me.

As well she might as things were to turn out.

Chapter 21

Somehow I've managed to prepare breakfast on auto-pilot. Those hazy images from the 1970s are whirling around in my mind and combined with a body clock that is still set to Canada, everything feels weird and disconnected.

'Mum I meant to say something last night....'

Amy has just barged into the kitchen looking like she has stepped out of a fashion magazine. Make-up perfectly applied, hair washed and styled and wearing a blue fitted dress that I haven't seen before. As for me, I'm still in PJs and feeling like shit.

'Morning – you're looking very nice. New dress?'

'No I've had it for ages. Mum before I forget again, can you arrange for me to get some work experience on Cornwall Now?'

The subject matter throws me.

'Mum, are you listening?'

'Sorry Amy...say again...'

Amy raises her eyes to the ceiling in mock exasperation.

'Doh, *work experience*. I just wondered if you could arrange for me to do a stint on the magazine?'

The penny has finally dropped but I'm still confused – or bemused rather.

'But why do you want to work on Cornwall Now? I thought you'd got your heart set on getting into radio work?'

Amy gives out a sigh, and grabs one of the slices of toast I've just laid out.

'Well I've been thinking. I'd like to give print a go, just to see what it's about. I was talking to someone who works in radio and she said that it's good to start off in print, that way you learn a lot about interviewing.'

I suppose she is right. I know plenty of people who have made the transition from print to broadcasting but so far Amy has never really shown a great interest in written journalism.

'If you're serious about doing it then I'll run it past my editor Elaine' I reply, adding that I can't give any guarantees.

'But you get on really well with Elaine, why would she say no?' Amy asks, before taking a large - and clearly irritated - bite from her toast.

She's right, I do get on with Elaine, and even more so since she revealed that she knew David's strumpet, Jemma. As it turned out, she had actually worked for Elaine before moving on to the Echo newspaper where she met David.

He was only her boss, damn it.

Still, I don't want to put Elaine on the spot and I'm not even sure that it's a good idea for Amy to work at the same place as me.

'Anyway, we're only talking about a couple of weeks mum. I could hang out with Kevin and just do the odd day or two with you.' My girl is persistent, I'll give her that. Not a bad trait if she does want to go the journalism route.

'Look, I said I'd talk to Elaine so let's just leave it at that. I'll be seeing her tomorrow. Now do you want coffee...?'

Amy nods, realising that she isn't going to get a straight 'yes' from me about the job experience however hard she pushes.

A phone call from Ashley distracts her long enough for me to get dressed and make myself presentable. It also gives me time to make an excuse to my neighbour, Ted, that I'm far too jet-lagged to see him today. He takes it well reminding me that his latest 'lady friend' is whisking him off him off to lunch later. I've lost count of Ted's very own harem but however many there are, he's looking sprightlier by the day. Good on him.

Ashley turns out to be a real surfer boy personified. He's taller and more muscular than I expected from his photos and has unruly wheat coloured wavy hair. In some ways he reminds me of a younger David and I can see straight away why Amy is attracted to him.

'Debbie – we finally meet then.' He puts out his hand and we exchange an awkward overly polite shake.

'Oh for goodness sake you two, have a proper hug!' Amy says, pushing Ashley forward. Ashley laughs sheepishly as he puts his arms around me and I respond with a nervous giggle. Talk about embarrassing.

The awkwardness doesn't last long though. For his age Ashley is remarkably self confident and assured. A bit over the top polite at times but that is probably his public school background.

Amy manages to bring the conversation back around to my lack of photographs from my Canada trip.

'Doh, can you believe she lost her camera?' she mocks, giving me a playful push.

'Take no notice Debbie, it happens loads – I'm always losing stuff' Ashley replies, before regaling us with tales of lost phones, a computer and a number of suitcases.

'I even lost my sister once when we were little. I was supposed to be looking after her and she slipped out of my sight. It wasn't for long but mum was furious.'

'I can see that I'll have to keep an eye on you' Amy adds, throwing her arm around Ashley's broad shoulders. Suddenly I feel a bit like a gooseberry, wondering whether I should just leave them alone for a while.

'Debbie, do you want to join us for later for a meal?' Ashley asks, fixing his greenish-grey eyes on me. My, those eyes really are something else.

Distracted, I look across at Amy to suss her reaction. Do these love birds really want me tagging along? Amy looks non-plussed, clearly not minding one way or the other.

'Oh thanks Ashley but perhaps some other time. You two go ahead and maybe we can go out somewhere tomorrow if you like?'

If I'm not mistaken, I think I've called it right - at least as far as Amy is concerned. We leave things that I'll treat them to dinner tomorrow and tonight I'll have some quiet time in while they go off clubbing.

As Amy disappears to fine tune her already perfect make-up, Ashley takes the opportunity to tell me how fond he is of her.

'And I can see where Amy gets her good looks from' he says, appearing for all the world that he means it. Not usually the type to be bothered about compliments, I'm relishing this one. From someone else it might sound like a cheesy 'wanting to get in your good books' line but I don't get any sense that Ashley is the bullshitting type. Far from it in fact.

After they leave, I find myself staring again at Mr DJ's photos. Clearly they are duplicates of the originals, and the colours faded with white age specks giving the impression of a light fluttering of snow across some of them.

Future generations will never have this problem with digital memories captured forever in pristine shape. Perfect and beautifully formed.

Some might even say clinical. Not a word you could use about these decades-old snap shots.

Shots of a world long gone but with events still playing out in the 21st century.

Messy, complicated and imperfect.

My life history in a nutshell.

Chapter 22

There is a saying that you should never work with animals or children. I'd add to that, 'especially your *own* children.'

Amy got her way as she usually does. Despite my misgivings about her joining 'Cornwall Now' for work experience, she did exactly that - in the busy run up to Christmas to boot.

It all went hunky dory to start with. Amy worked alongside Kevin and was a useful extra pair of hands as he recovered from his broken ankle. Now that Kevin had pretty much moved in with us, they'd have long post mortems about page layouts and designs after work. Good for their own relationship bonding, but certainly not for ours.

Then there was the office Christmas party and the start of everything going wrong. And I mean it when I use the word 'everything'.

To say that Amy looked stunning in her party outfit barely does it justice. When she eventually emerged from her bedroom, Kevin and me were speechless. She was wearing a short red sparkly dress that clung to every curve and flattered her size 10 figure to a 'T'. A pair of uber-high slingback heels accentuated her long legs and unusually her hair was piled upwards into a structured sixties style bun. Even her make-up was worthy of a professional. She could have stepped out of the pages of Vogue and boy did she know it.

'Wow Amy – you look incredible.' Kevin was the first to speak with me still gobstruck, hardly able to believe that this was my little girl.

Amy did a quick twirl, waiting for my approval.

'Yes, you do look stunning' I finally remarked, wishing that I'd made a bit more effort with my own outfit. Too late now though.

'Hey you look great as well mum' Amy replied, giving me a hug and with it came a waft of my favourite bottle of Chanel perfume.

Then off we went to the Christmas party, with me feeling every bit like a dowdy aunt at a wedding. Presentable but no more than that.

Predictably Amy was the proverbial belle of the ball. She got a lot of male attention all right and from one in particular. My boss Carl Martin. Yes, Amy had certainly caught the eye of Mr Editorial Director.

To be fair, it all seemed pretty harmless at first. Everyone had lots to drink with the usual work party teasing and banter. Once I started to relax, it even began to feel like a bit of fun.

Then I started to notice that Amy had barely left Carl's side. They were deep in conversation, laughing and clearly enjoying each other's company. I could tell that Carl liked what he saw and more worryingly, so did Amy.

Part of me wanted to barge over and remind my daughter that she had a lovely boyfriend who was due to join us for Christmas. Then again, my more sensible inner voice told me to cool it – it was just a bit of harmless party fun, replicated in offices all over the country.

'Looks like Carl has really taken a shine to Amy' Kevin joked, handing me a large glass of winter Pimms.

'I can see that' I snapped back, trying but failing miserably to hide my irritation. Kevin knew only too well not to continue the conversation and still hobbling on his broken ankle, he moved forward and gave me a passionate hug. It was a clear signal to anyone at work who didn't already know. We were now officially - and without apology - a couple, there for all to see.

Of course I laughed and gave him a playful wag of my finger. All the time keeping my eyes fixed on Amy and Carl.

By 1am I'd had enough of the workplace bonhomie and suggested to Kevin that we call it a night. Amy though was having none of it. She was enjoying herself far too much to go home, so told us that she'd make her own way back.

Just before I left, I pulled her to one side. Carl had gone to get them both another drink so it was my chance to pounce.

'You and Carl seem to be glued together' I remarked, trying to sound breezy, devil-may-care.

'Mum he's lush – a really interesting guy. You're so lucky to work with him.'

'Well watch yourself with him' I replied, immediately regretting my choice of words.

Amy raised her eyes to the ceiling.

'Mum, what are you like? I can look after myself. I'm not a baby anymore.'

'No but you have a boyfriend and I'm not sure what he'd make of your flirting.'

Again I'd used the wrong words but couldn't help myself. Blame it on the Christmas booze fest.

'Ah Debbie. Are you off already?' Out of nowhere, Carl appeared with two glasses of champagne and looking as dapper as ever despite the late hour.

'Yes, I'm afraid so' I responded sheepishly, hoping that he hadn't overheard my last comment to Amy. Meanwhile madam gave me a long stare, making it clear that she wasn't happy.

'I've been enjoying the chat with your lovely daughter' Carl said, smiling across at Amy. 'I think she's got a good future in magazine journalism if she wants it. Takes after her talented mum.'

He meant it as a compliment but to my ears it sounded like patronising claptrap. Time for a sharp exit and to cross my fingers that Amy really did know how to handle herself – and him.

As the saying goes, I made my excuses and left. Kevin had already hailed a taxi and was waiting outside, clutching a half-drunken beer in one hand while he steadied himself on his crutch with the other.

'Ah, here comes my beautiful Debbie' he said, slightly slurring his words. But I wasn't in the mood for his lovey-dovey playfulness. Not with my daughter in the clutches of Mr Dynamic just a few feet away.

As I said before, this was the night where everything started to unravel.

The night when my daughter came face-to-face with her late father's treachery.

Chapter 23

After getting back from the party, we sat up into the early hours discussing our future together. It was the intimate chat we were supposed to be having in New York, in a romantic hotel with a glorious panoramic view of that great city. Hey ho, Truro will have to do instead.

'Are you sure you want to move in permanently?' I ask, the question really aimed at me as much as Kevin.

'Of course – you know I do. We're a great team aren't we?' Kevin means well but I flinch at that word 'team'. It sounds workman-like, functional and the pole opposite of romantic.

As I sip my coffee, I'm staring pointedly at him. Is this what I really want too? Am I rushing things as an angry reaction to David, a sort of kick in a dead man's teeth?

As if reading my mind, Kevin pulls me towards him, taking my face in his hand.

'Never mind me. This is really about you isn't it?'

I nod and no more words are needed. Sealed with a kiss as they say, and a long passionate one at that. It's good to have the house to ourselves for a few hours and any thoughts of Amy and Carl are pushed well into the background.

We don't hear her arrive home but she's up early the next morning ready for work with no sign of a hangover.

'Come on Kevin we'll be late.' She's standing in the hallway, part-eaten cereal bar in one hand and an energy drink in the other. When she sees me I get a steely glare as a reminder that no, she hasn't forgotten what I said last night. Far from it.

'What time did you get back?' I ask, ignoring the childish sulk.

She sniffs, pointedly checking her watch before answering.

'3 o'clockish if you must know. And no I didn't go back to Carl's place if that's what you're thinking.'

'That's not what I was thinking. Did you all go on to a club?' I'm trying to sound conciliatory but she's having none of it.

'No we didn't actually. We stayed put and some people from the Echo newspaper joined us.' Again she's checking her watch, looking over my shoulder for a sign of Kevin.

'Stop staring at your watch, he'll be down in a minute. No one will care if you are a few minutes late today.'

Meanwhile my mind is in a spin over the Echo staff.

'Er, who came from the paper then...?' I ask, as if it's a mere after thought.

'Oh I dunno – someone called Jack who is a reporter, the editor Trevor and a few people from sales. They were all quite a laugh.'

A few people from sales. That's all I've heard. A few people from sales.

'Who was there from sales?' I ask, as nonchalantly as I can muster.

'Bloody hell mum what's with all the questions? I can't remember everyone but there was a nice guy called Tim I think and someone called Jemma.'

Shit. The name I was dreading.

'The names don't mean much to me – although I think Elaine mentioned someone called Jemma once....'

Amy isn't listening as she's just spotted Kevin emerging from the kitchen.

'Ah at last we're off' she says sarcastically, rolling her eyes upwards.

'You're keen this morning' Kevin replies, a knowing twinkle in his eye. 'Anything to do with someone called Carl?'

Not the right thing to say given Amy's mood this morning.

'What is it with you two about Carl? He's a nice guy, we get on. End of. Now come on Kevin, we should really be going.'

A perfunctory kiss from him – certainly different from last night – and a sullen wave from Amy and they're off. With me left wondering whether Amy and Jemma actually got to speak. The thought makes me feel sick.

I can't hang around all day guessing, so there's no choice. I'll have to call Elaine right now – I'm due to meet an up-and-coming fashion designer later this morning and won't be in the office until the afternoon. There's no way I'm waiting that long to get the low down on last night's encounter with the minx I haven't even met yet. Time to put that right soon.

Elaine isn't too pleased to be woken from her post party lie-in.

'Hell Debbie you certainly pick your time. I was in a lovely deep sleep...' She yawns loudly to make her point. As for me I'm raring to go.

'Sorry Elaine. But I'm off in an hour and I've had a bit of a shock this morning...'

'You all right? You sound in a bit of a panic...Kevin's OK isn't he?'

'Yes he's fine. It's Amy actually – she said something about the Echo team joining you at the party last night.'

'Oh did they? Must have been after I sloped off then.'

'And Amy mentioned that Jemma was there.'

'Oh – bloody hell Debbie. I can see why you're

worried.' She clears her throat, more out of awkwardness than anything else.

'Yeh, right. The thing is Elaine, I don't know whether they got to talk. Shit! If they did... Amy was in a funny mood this morning.'

Elaine stays silent for a few moments, weighing up the possibility.

'Look the place was packed by the time I left and the chances are they didn't even get to speak. Even if they did, it was probably just a few passing words – I doubt if either of them had a clue about their...er...shared links to David.'

She's probably right of course. Still, I need a bit more reassurance.

'Could you ask around this morning for me? I'll be in later but I could do with knowing before then.'

'I suppose so but I'm sure I'm right about this. You could hardly hear yourself speak over the music later on – that's why I left. Trust me, I wouldn't angst too much Debbie.'

'It's just that she mentioned Jemma by name' I reply, only partly comforted by Elaine's take on things.

'Yes well – you don't see Jemma without remembering her. Anyway, I'll ask around and I'll get back to you one way or the other.'

One way or the other. Let's just hope it's the other.

Chapter 24

Christmas has been and gone in a blur but we managed to enjoy ourselves, with Kevin juggling his time between us and visiting his boys. I even got to speak with Andy on Christmas Eve, a leisurely chat while Kevin and Amy were out scouting for last minute presents. He sounded happy and was looking forward to his skiing trip with Lauren – the one where he would present his engagement ring.

'Hey - happy Christmas Debbie. Isn't it strange to think that this time last year we didn't even know where either of us lived?' We stay quiet for a few moments, both pondering the changes in our lives since then. It's Andy who breaks the silence.

'You know the patient I told you about, the one who was trying to contact his birth parents? He died just a few days after last Christmas.'

We both understand the significance of this, the reason why Andy decided to contact me. He didn't want to be that man in thirty years' time, battling a terminal illness and desperately trying to get information about his own flesh and blood.

'Happy Christmas Andy.'

He can't see it but the tears are rolling down my

cheeks as I find myself staring once again at photos of the 16 year old me, the ones sent by Mr DJ. A mixture of gauche and knowing, the same look that Amy has these days.

In the end I did send off Christmas cards to Andy and Mr DJ. A catch-all family one for Andy – I couldn't bring myself to buy a 'son' card for fear of upsetting Theresa and Joe – and one featuring a retro jukebox for Mr DJ. In it I thanked him for sending the photos and said that I'd be back in touch in the new year, when he's home from his winter sun break in Tenerife.

And yes I've made up my mind to write that letter, even if it is the last one I ever send him.

As for life on the home front, it still seems strange having a man living with us again but at least Kevin and Amy are getting on brilliantly. We're now in that funny time between Christmas and New Year and today I've got the house back to myself. Kevin is working on the next magazine issue and Amy is staying at Ashley's family home for a few days.

It seems that Elaine had been right all along to say that I shouldn't get in a panic over Jemma coming to the office Christmas party. From what she could pick up, Carl and Amy hit the dance floor after we left and pretty much stayed there until the party ended at 2pm. By then the Echo sales staff had already gone and no one noticed any chat going on between Jemma and Amy. I still feel uneasy about the encounter but in the circumstances there is not much I can do about it.

Meantime Carl seems to have taken Amy under his wing and for her final work placement weeks she'll be working alongside him. Of course I'll be around from time to time to keep an eye on her and can't help feeling uneasy about their growing closeness.

Oversensitivity because of my own history? Kevin certainly thinks so and yes, he's right on that score.

Still, I've managed to do a bit more digging on Jemma Atkins and I've discovered that we are both due to be at a marketing conference in a few weeks time. By then Amy will be back at University and it gives me time to think about how I should introduce myself to my late husband's mistress.

'Hi Jemma – it's me Debbie McKay. You know, wife of David.... remember him?'

As I mentally rehearse my introduction, I'm staring at her latest website picture. She's changed it recently, along with her hair colour which is now light brown instead of bleach blonde. It actually suits her better, softening her features and flattering what looks like a post-holiday tan. When I first saw her photo, I didn't think she looked as pretty as Elaine had described her. Now though, I can see why she had Elaine's sales team wrapped around her finger and how she got her clutches into David.

It's strange but I don't even feel all that angry any more. Sad, but not the red mist of anger that I had when I originally found out. It's a good sign that I'm moving on, the distraction of a new relationship with Kevin, meeting my son and a change of job, all playing a part here. Oh, and Mr DJ's advice on the matter of course.

As I dig deeper, Jemma is all over social media like a rash. From what I can see there's no obvious serious relationship – just lots of pictures of friends having fun, often mucking around in 'selfie' shots. For someone who is still in her twenties, her professional CV looks quite impressive. I can see that she's recently had a promotion to senior sales executive, the job David had when we first got together. Her direct work line is also out there in all its tempting glory.

Hell, I can't resist the urge to ring it, just to hear her voice. Gearing up to pose as someone wanting to place an advertisement, it's disappointing just to get the answer machine.

'Hello this is Jemma. I'm sorry I'm not available to talk at the moment but do leave a message and I'll get back as quickly as I can. Alternatively you can email me through the company website.'

Her voice is confident, with no distinctive accent. A bit girly and sing-songy, going up a few notches at the end like a lot of young people – Amy included. This upward inflection at the end of sentences drives me nuts as it sounds so phoney. US valley-speak meets Aussie soap stars.

Of course I don't bother to leave a message but at

least I've got a measure of the voice. Anyway, by the time we get to meet, I'll know a lot more about Ms Atkins.

The poor girl won't have a clue that she's about to meet David's widow. Of course she would have found out about my existence after David died - assuming he hadn't already told her, which I'm convinced is the case. That must have come as hell of a shock.

But what she won't know is that I'm aware of their sordid little affair and I'll be acting as a 'post mistress' when I finally come face to face with her.

With a special delivery of her love notes and cards to my dead husband.

Now that should wipe the smile from her pretty little face.

Here's to the New Year and everything it brings.

Chapter 25

The best laid plans and all that. It seems to be my regular mantra. Just when you think you've got everything sorted, life comes and kicks you in the teeth. Big time.

What do they say about New Year, new beginning?

Having spent the past two weeks using every excuse I can to spy on my boss Carl and my daughter, it's finally Amy's last day on the magazine. To say I'm relieved is putting it mildly. Of course there's been the odd bit of flirting going on – largely on Amy's part – and it's obvious she has a huge crush on Carl.

But as far as I can tell, it is nothing more than that and to be fair, a good chunk of the Cornwall Now female staff have the hots for Carl. Maybe even some of the guys too for all I know. As for me, I can see the attraction but no more than that. He's like one of those glossy magazine models, good to look at but a bit too picture perfect. I'd rather have Kevin, dodgy ankle and all.

'Hey mum, Carl has suggested we go for a drink after work as it's my last day. Do you want to come?'

We're in the magazine reception area where I'm waiting for a delivery of a food hamper, a present from a grateful client. The rules are that we can accept a few gifts as long as they are shared out amongst the staff and food samples like these are always popular, with yours truly at the front of the queue.

'Er... me and Kevin are heading out for a pizza after work. What time were you thinking of?'

'Dunno. About 6 o'clock I suppose.' If I'm not mistaken, Amy is looking relieved.

'Is it just you two or is anyone else going?'

Amy pauses for a few seconds and already I know the answer. It's just the two of them with mum being asked out of politeness.

'Carl didn't mention anyone else...but he did say to ask you.'

Hmm. Go and I'll just look like a saddo stalking my daughter. Don't go and my meal with Kevin will be ruined with worries about what my daughter's up to.

OK, the last option it is. Better than being a mad mamma stalker and I should really trust Amy a bit more. After all, she's already got a regular boyfriend and she'll be heading back to him any day now.

'No you two just go on your own – me and Kevin will catch up with you later.'

Amy gives me a quick hug, a clear substitute for the word 'phew'.

'Ah thanks mum. I expect it won't be a long drink – you know how busy Carl is.'

Indeed I do. How he manages to juggle all his work projects is a mystery to me. But juggle things he does and I've never once seen him lose his temper.

'Have a good time and here – buy Carl a drink with this.'

I hand her a twenty pound note which she takes with a gleeful 'ah thanks mum, you're the best.'

If only.

It's now 2am and Kevin is snoring lightly. I did make an effort not to think about Amy and Carl during what turned out to be an enjoyable meal. After getting home we decided to watch a trashy film and by the time it finished we were both ready to hit the sack.

Still no sign of Amy though and no text to say she'd be late.

'Stuff it, I'll ring her mobile.' When I uttered these words Kevin gave me one of his 'go on then but I think you're being a bit over the top' looks. Of course I ignored it and called her mobile anyway. No reply, just her usual answer message.

'Hi darling. Just to let you know that we're off to bed, so we'll see you in the morning. Hope you are having a good time, love you lots.' There, done and dusted but it didn't make me feel any better.

That was three hours ago and I've checked my

phone several times for text messages but so far nothing. Kevin's comment, just before he fell asleep, was that if Amy was back at university then I wouldn't be worrying. For all I know she could be out all hours of the night on a regular basis. 'It's called growing up' he said. But she's not at university and she's still – as far as I know – out with my boss, damn it.

Hang on, isn't that her key being pushed into the door? Thank the Lord.

I could pretend to be asleep, trusting and unconcerned. That's not me though.

Within seconds I'm in the kitchen and Amy is slumped at the table, her head in her hands.

'Amy – is everything all right?'

I've startled her and when she stares back at me I can see that she's been crying.

'Darling – what on earth is the matter?'

She's still staring at me, tearful but there's something else. Frustration, anger or perhaps both.

'Why did you keep asking me questions about the Echo sales people coming to the Christmas party?'

Her question throws me and instead of moving over to comfort her, I'm rooted to the spot.

'Did I? I don't remember...'

'Oh come on mum. You remember all right. Why did you ask?'

I'm lost for words and can feel my mouth drying

'You kept asking about a woman called Jemma – does that ring a bell?'

Of course it does and she damn well knows it.

'Well funnily enough I met Jemma again tonight. She turned up at the same pub as me and Carl. In fact we ended up having quite a chat.'

Oh shit. I can feel the colour drain from my face and my heart starting to race.

'Yeh we got on well and when I told her my surname was McKay, she went quiet for a few minutes and then said that she once had an older boyfriend called David McKay. That's right. David. McKay.'

I'm listening but it's as if I'm having one of those out-of-body experiences people talk about. I'm standing there but also peering across at the scene as if I were watching a movie. Yes, that feature film of my life.

Amy is now looking straight ahead, at something in the far distance. I know what's coming next. Oh god.

'Mum she was speaking about dad.'

She's staring back at me, reading my face for any sign that I know what she is on about. There's no hiding the answer either.

'Yes darling...it was your dad.'

If this were really a film, she'd look shocked or

even let out a scream.

Instead there is silence, a seemingly long one. Then the words, icy calm but angry and accusing.

'So you knew all along. That's why you kept on about Jemma being at the party. Mum how could you not say anything? '

Words come from my mouth but my body is still elsewhere. Floating somewhere above, eyeing the scene with an unnerving detachment. Some might even call it shock.

'I haven't known for long Amy. Trust me.'

She scoffs at the mention of the word trust.

'Long enough not to say anything to me, your own daughter.'

I jump as she pushes the table hard across the kitchen, the scraping noise echoing across the room.

'Mum I want to know the truth. Don't you dare keep me in the dark anymore. He was my dad...'

I want to comfort her, I really do. But the table is strewn in front of me, a physical barrier between mother and daughter. In the background I can hear Kevin moving around upstairs – he'll be down here any minute.

'OK Amy, calm down. I'll tell you everything, promise.'

As I said, the best laid plans. Scuppered in the worst way possible and I hardly know where to begin.

Chapter 26

Voices - Amy...

Hi there, this is Amy speaking. You've not heard directly from me yet but you are about to. Big time.

Now what sort of mother finds out that her dead husband was cheating on her and keeps it from her own daughter? That man was my dad, the one I still miss every day, the one who was taken away so brutally without warning.

It was the day of my English exam, a hot early summer day. I left the house in the morning still with a living, breathing dad and just few hours later I was being driven home by the head teacher. No dad anymore and a mum who could barely speak.

I suppose that was the day I grew up, the day I became a fully fledged adult, looking out for mum and pretending that I didn't hear her sobbing every evening. For a while I was on auto pilot, trying to be the stronger one while deep inside I longed to retreat back into my childhood cocoon, safe and sound. Dad's music was my only solace and I'd play his old LPs over and over. In the past I would have dissed his choice of bands, moaning about having to put up with saddo dad rock. I knew mum was upset

153

when I played an old favourite of his but I couldn't help myself. While the music played he was there, lounging on the sofa and nodding his head to the beat. It was my time to cry, to try to come to terms with his death, in the only way I knew.

We muddled along for a while, mum and me, creating our own little bubble and nursing our pain. When one of us was down, the other played the supporting role and little-by-little we blinked back into the daylight. Our grief was always there, flaring up without warning but we kept each other going, mum and me.

That's why this is so hard to take. Not once did I believe that my mum could discover something as shocking as this and not say anything. To hide it away, hoping - I suppose - that I'd never find out.

Well I found out all right, and what a way to discover that the dad you loved to bits was leading a secret life. Shagging someone else behind our backs, a girl not that much older than me.

I've been replaying the conversation with Jemma – if you can even call it a 'conversation' – over and over, like one of dad's old LPs. It may not be word perfect but it is close enough, piercing my brain like a white hot brand.

Everything started out innocently enough. Carl suggested that we go to Billy's Bar, the new trendy place just a short walk from work. I'd enjoyed working with Carl, a really cool guy with a great brain and bod to match. I know mum was worried that we were getting too close but then with her generation, it's always about sex. I think she'd been secretly reading that 50 Shades book, expecting Carl to behave like Christian Grey with me cast as Anastacia. As if I'd be so stupid, or him for that matter.

No, ours was just a meeting of minds with a little bit of harmless flirting to make things fun. My generation can accept that kind of friendship for what it is. I'm more grown up than mum thinks, with far more common sense than she gives me credit for and besides, I've already fallen head over heels for Ashley.

Anyway, as you already know, I've jumped several massive hoops to get to the adult stage in double-quick time.

So we get to Billy's and it's a busy place, the happy hour cocktail deals drawing the younger crowd in. Mine was a large vodka and cranberry juice and Carl went for his favourite whisky sour. I can even recall the conversation just before my life imploded.

'So your mum didn't fancy joining us then?' He was eyeing me with a mix of amusement as I tried to pull out the strawberry from my drink and with the sort of flirtatiousness that is typical of Carl off-duty. The man works hard but knows when to leave the serious stuff at the door.

'No and I'm cool about that. I didn't fancy mum hanging around.'

I managed to extract the strawberry and pop it into my mouth, Carl laughing at my childish gesture. What's the point of putting fruit in a drink if you don't bother to eat it?

That's when Jemma waltzed in, wearing sprayed on white jeans and black knee-high suede boots. Topped by a biker's style leather jacket she looked amazing.

'Carl – sorry I'm late. The meeting went on longer than we expected.'

As they exchanged kisses, I recognised her from the Christmas party. She was with a group of colleagues from the local newspaper and they were all pretty drunk from what I could remember.

So how come Carl hadn't mentioned her joining us? They seem like good friends, perhaps even a bit more from the look of things.

'This is Amy who has been with us on a work placement.' Carl smiled as he introduced me and Jemma held out her hand. Obviously she didn't remember me from the party.

We shook hands awkwardly and Carl offered to buy her a drink. Clearly he knew her well enough not to have to ask what drink she wanted. As for me, I was just a little intern who had no say in the matter.

To be fair, she turned out to be good company and seemed genuinely interested in hearing about my time at 'Cornwall Now', adding that she'd loved her time working there. While Carl popped outside to answer a call on his mobile, she gave me a playful nudge.

'Hey – Carl's pretty shit hot isn't he?'

I remember blushing, not quite knowing how to respond.

'Tell you what Amy, he's a guy going places.'

That's when we got onto the subject of my surname.

'Let me have your phone number and email so we can keep in touch.' Jemma was already keying my name into her phone, all the time keeping one eye out for Carl's return.

'What's your last name then?'

'McKay – m-c-k-a-y' I replied, spelling it out.

Jemma looked up at me, and her expression could best be described as quizzical.

'McKay – funny, that was the name of a former boyfriend of mine.'

It was my turn to look surprised. It's not a common name, certainly not in this part of the country.

'Oh that's a coincidence – did he live in Truro?'

Jemma looked down, her look changing from bemusement to sadness.

'Yes he did. He died just over four years ago.'

I couldn't believe it. Not only was he called

McKay but he died at the very same time as my dad.

'What was his full name?' Even as I asked the question, I knew what was coming. Oh God, surely not.

Jemma paused for a few moments and I could see that she was getting upset.

'David'.

No, no, no.

'That was my dad's name. He died then too.'

I could see the change on Jemma's face as she took in the information. There was no escape route for her. There she was, face-to-face with her dead boyfriend's daughter.

'I think I'd better go'. As the words came out of my mouth, I knew that if I didn't make my escape right then, there was no accounting for what I would do.

'Hang on Amy...at least let me...' I didn't let her finish the sentence before grabbing my bag and heading to the exit.

Carl was standing outside, his back to me as he talked into his phone. I didn't bother to interrupt him but just fled down the road, not sure where I was going.

How on earth was I going to tell mum? I'd have to tell her, it's not something that I'd be able to keep to myself.

I jumped as my mobile phone rang out. It was

Carl, wondering where I had gone. Jemma had told him that I'd just set off, clearly not mentioning the reason why.

I tried to sound casual, as if running away part way through a night out with your boss was the most natural thing in the world.

'Sorry Carl. I didn't want to interrupt your call but I just heard from my boyfriend Ashley. He's on his way down to Truro – he'll be getting here any minute.'

'Oh well just get him to join us back here if you want to.' If only things were that simple.

I thanked him for the offer and then made some lame excuse about Ashley not liking bars.

'Really? Well keep in touch and pop in to see me before you head back to university,' Carl replied, sounding pretty gracious in the circumstances.

'Thank you for everything Carl. I've enjoyed working with you.'

And that was that. I made my way down to the Lemon Quay area of the city and sat on a bench near the bus station.

My phone rang out again and this time it was from Jemma. She must have managed to key in my details before the surname debacle. I ignored the call but saved her details to my phone for future reference.

Then I remembered mum's questions about Jemma after the Christmas party. How she kept asking about her, what we'd chatted about.

Not much as it happened, we barely exchanged words that night and she was too full of booze to remember me. Yet mum kept banging on about her for some reason.

Then the penny dropped. Or clanged more like.

Mum knew. She must have. That's why she was so bothered about Jemma and me meeting up. What other explanation could there be?

That's when I started to cry, silent tears followed by heavier sobs.

'Hey – what's wrong?'

A kindly elderly man stood over me, not sure whether to sit down on the bench.

'Oh just some family trouble,' I replied, dabbing my eyes with a sodden tissue.

'Do you want to talk about it? My wife's just gone to buy a paper but we can take you for a cup of tea if you like.'

He was such a sweet guy but no, I needed to deal with this on my own.

I thanked him for his concern and told him I'd be fine. Really.

Then I jumped on a bus heading to who knows where. I just needed time to think and come to terms with the second biggest bombshell of my life.

After my dad's death that is.

Chapter 27

Voices - Jemma...

Let me introduce myself. It's Jemma here and it's time for you to hear my part of the story.

Oh shit.

Holy frigging shit. I can't believe that I've just spoken to David's daughter. How could I have been so stupid? Of course I knew nothing of his family's existence when we were an item and trust me, I'd never have got involved if I had.

Laughing? Well you don't scoff because it's true.

First the pain of his death and then finding out that he had a wife and teenage daughter. That was as shocking as him dying and of course I couldn't attend the actual the funeral service. How could I?

The family were as much in the dark as me, at least it seemed that way. After the funeral I hung around outside the church hoping to get a glimpse of them. I only saw them for a few seconds before they got into the funeral car and they were clinging on to each other for dear life. Mum and daughter oblivious to the betrayal of the man they were mourning. Suddenly I felt sick and threw up at the side of the road.

After that I went away for a while, telling my new boss that I needed a sabbatical to get over the sudden death of my 'colleague'. Little did he know just how close David and I had got, planning our first holiday together and talking about buying a flat. Like I said, none of this would have happened if he'd told me the frigging truth. Instead I believed him when he said that he'd split up with his wife years before and that they didn't have children.

Stupid bitch I hear you say. Yeah, stupid all right but there are plenty like me out there. Guilty of the crime of believing, falling in love with a lying cheating rat. Don't speak ill of the dead? Stuff that in your pipe and smoke it as my granddad used to say.

When I found out, I couldn't get my head around the risks he was taking. A wife and daughter living in the same city for pity's sake. We could have bumped into each other on any number of occasions.

I'd no idea that Debbie McKay was the 'Cornwall Now' feature writer 'Debbie Clark' because back then she was still using her unmarried name in her by-line.

Amazingly, no one at our office mentioned that David was even married. I suppose they just assumed that I knew. Yet the news could have come out at any point. Come to think of it, I was always out on the road and hardly ever in the office. When I was there, it was to meet David and as things progressed he tried to join me on my trips away as much as possible.

Still, the risks he took. Did he enjoy the thrill of being too close for comfort? It was probably the strain of this constant deceit that did for him in the end. The stress must have been intolerable yet he never showed any signs of this to me. Far from it in fact.

Our last night together seems just like yesterday. We checked into a favourite spa hotel on the outskirts of Falmouth, trashing the bed with our frenzied love-making and just about getting down to the dining room before they stopped serving. David said he had to hit the road in the early hours of the next morning for an important meeting with a client in Gloucestershire. We made love once more before he set off and that was it. My last sight of David was him waving across the room and mouthing that he loved me.

Then the call. It was our deputy manager, James, asking me if I'd heard the tragic news. I'd pulled over to the side of the road and for a moment I thought I was the victim of a stupid sick prank. David dead? How could that be?

Then the questions. Where? When? What? I said that I thought David was in Gloucestershire and he assured me that no, he had gone into work and was due to chair a meeting at 10am. When David didn't turn up, James went to see if his car was there and it was. David was inside, slumped across the steering wheel. I could hear the crack in his voice as he described opening the car door and realising that something was badly wrong.

'His poor wife and daughter are in bits Jemma.'

Wife and daughter? It took me another few seconds to digest this news.

'Jemma - you still there...?' James's voice cut back in like a sharpened knife.

'Er yes, sorry. It's just that I can't quite take this in.' Sudden death and a family who were still on the scene. My brain had gone into a tail spin.

James suggested that I take the rest of the day off and promised to ring my client to explain. The next few days were spent in a blur trying to juggle loss with a deep sense of betrayal. When I wasn't crying, I was screaming at the photograph of us taken just a few weeks before. On the day that he told me that he wanted us to spend the rest of our lives together.

Taking a year out to travel to Australia and Thailand was a wise decision and helped to ease the pain. Once back in England, I returned to my old job and decided to make it the focus of my life. Relationships could wait - that's if I could ever trust anyone again.

Then Mr Carl Martin came along. I'd met him briefly at a marketing conference in London and was impressed. Enough so to go out for a drink with him and mark him down as someone to watch.

A few years later, who should turn up as the new

Editorial Director of Cornwall Now? You guessed it - Carl. Of course I made sure that I went for a second drink with him and we even talked about me moving back to the magazine – the last time I was there it was as a mere trainee.

The second drink led to a third and then progressed to a meal. Without giving too much away, I told Carl about my relationship with a married man and its sudden and tragic end. He was a good listener and I could feel myself letting go of the cast iron guard I'd built around myself over the past few years. At least a good frigging chunk of it.

'You have to learn to trust again Jemma. Take in the lesson life has thrown at you and then move on.'

I took that advice and Carl is now my mentor. And occasional lover. Nothing too serious this time. Just two adults having a bit of fun.

If only I'd straight gone home after that stupid work meeting, then I might never have discovered who Amy was. Sometimes ignorance really is bliss.

After she fled into the night, I learned from Carl that his newly appointed editorial events manager was Amy's mum. Shit what an unholy mess. Just as life seemed to be taking a turn for the better, this has to happen. If you believe in Karma, I must have been one hell of a bitch in a former life.

Tell Carl the truth? If I do he'll run a mile and who could blame him?

Sneaking off to the ladies, I tried to ring Amy. No reply. I couldn't bring myself to leave a message.

Carl joked that he'd never been stood up by two women before, after I feigned a migraine and told him that I needed to get home.

'Ah well – an early night will do me good', he quipped as I kissed him goodnight before jumping into a taxi.

Then I sent Amy a text. The message was simple.

'Please call me.'

Chapter 28

Voices - Andy...

My turn to speak now. Andy that is, Debbie's son and Dr Andrew Wilson to my patients.

So far you've only heard from me through my birth mother – my real mom and dad are the ones who brought me up, who took care of me as a child and saw me safely into adulthood. They are the ones I truly love.

Don't get me wrong though, I'm already extremely fond of Debbie and not for one second do I regret contacting her. I'd no idea what to expect or even if she'd want to talk to me. At one point I wasn't even sure if she was still alive.

The first sound of her voice is something I'll remember forever. Then the meeting in London and me desperately trying to hold it together. As the saying goes, "big boys don't cry" - except they do. I'm always telling my patients to confront their emotions, that holding back on them is neither good for physical or mental health. Easier said than done though, like a lot of things we doctors advise.

That first meeting left me elated and at the same

time confused. There was the niggling worry about upsetting my adoptive parents, even though they assured me that I was doing the right thing. Then there's a half-sister of mine, Amy, who I might never get to meet and a birth father who Debbie says she knows nothing about.

My girlfriend Lauren, isn't convinced about this last bit.

'Come on Andy, do you really believe that....*really*...?' she asked after her first encounter with Debbie.

Her comment threw me because in all honesty, I did believe what Debbie had said. These things can happen and the story of a drunken tryst at a party, kind of made sense. Not a nice sort of sense, but it had a ring of truth about it. Anyway, why would she lie?

'All sorts of reasons,' Lauren replied when I said as much.

'Like what...?'

'Like she wants to protect him for some reason or doesn't want her family to know who he is. Maybe he isn't even alive anymore...' Lauren, the psychologist I love to bits, has raised her doubts.

As for me, I'm happy as things stand. I've met my birth mom and that's enough for me. OK, it would be great to know who my birth dad is or was, but it's not something I'm going to dwell on.

'Andy I have to tell you this – promise now you

won't be upset.' Lauren had snuggled up to me on the sofa, the night before she was due to head off on a four day work course.

I tweaked her nose and did a mock 'scouts honour' sign.

'Well, I like Debbie, she's your other mom after all, but I can sense she's not telling the whole story about her life.'

I didn't reply and truth is I felt irritated. Why couldn't Lauren just be happy for me? This has been a big deal and Lauren raising these doubts isn't being helpful.

'You're annoyed now aren't you?' she asked, looking crestfallen.

'No not annoyed, just...confused that's all. You've only met her once.' I sounded defensive and Lauren knew it.

'Look, we've always said we'd be honest with each other didn't we?' Lauren was staring hard at me with her beautiful, soulful eyes.

I nodded, trying look like the loving boyfriend I was.

'And that's why I feel I've got to share my thoughts. I'm the most disconnected one in the family, more the outsider if you like. So I can be more detached.'

That's when Lauren told me why she believed Debbie was holding back something. The body language when Lauren had raised the question about my birth father, the awkward eye movements when she pushed this a bit further. Hadn't I noticed this myself, she asked?

Yes, I had noticed that Debbie had looked uncomfortable at times during that first meeting with Lauren but I put it down to nervousness. As much as I love Lauren, she can be intimidating to those who don't really know her. Underneath, she's really quite shy and over compensates by being a bit brusque sometimes. Of course she doesn't mean to be, it's just how she can come across. Believe me when I tell you that the real Lauren is not like that.

Still, she's raised questions that weren't there before. But I'm still going to put them on the back burner and just concentrate on the here and now. After all, we've got a lot to celebrate haven't we?

Like me, mom and dad have just accepted what Debbie has told us and I'm not going to tell them about Lauren's doubts. I've asked her to keep it between ourselves and she's promised to do just that.

My folks find Debbie delightful and would like us all to stay in touch. Mom confided in me that she'd love to meet Debbie's family one day, maybe travelling back to England to do so. Since my adopted grandpa died, mom and dad haven't been back to 'Blighty' as they call it.

They don't want to put Debbie under any pressure and neither do I, though the thought of meeting my half sister is an exciting one. I've seen her picture and she looks nothing like me - well maybe just a little bit around the eyes if you look closely. She has a feisty, attractive appearance and like Lauren, I imagine that she can hold her own in company. Debbie clearly loves her and there is no jealousy there on my part.

'Love' is too big a word to say yet about my relationship with Debbie. There's a bond, affection, a like-ability, but not the love I feel for mom and pa and Lauren. No, it's way too soon for that but things could change if our relationship goes further.

The next step then? I'm going to hand that over to Debbie. When she left Canada, she said she'd like to come back again and I know she's got a lot more thinking to do on that score. It will be for her and her alone to decide where we all go from here.

As for us, life goes on and the next big celebration will be my engagement to Lauren. She described herself as the 'outsider' in our family, but that's all due to change. She'll be entering into the inner Wilson family circle, with everything that entails.

And it will have to include an acceptance of Debbie, doubts or no doubts about her version of the past. That bit at least, is non-negotiable.

Chapter 29

Voices - Amy again...

It's me – Amy speaking. Last time you heard from me I'd just had a blazing row with my mum and now I'm in Penzance, right at the far west of Cornwall.

The station is empty but I've managed to find a nearby coffee shop that is still open.

I can barely remember the journey, as my mind is working overtime. Mum has rung several times and I know she must be worried. Tough. She should have thought about that when she kept quiet about my dad and what he'd been getting up to.

Yeh, I'm annoyed with him as well even though he's no longer around to answer for his actions. I mean, why did he need to screw around with another woman? He had me and mum and our lives were happy. Or so I thought. Shows how wrong you can be, even when you think you know those closest to you.

But it is mum I'm really mad at right now. I didn't think we had secrets and in many ways I've been more of the grown up one in our relationship.

Let's face it I've had to be and that's why her deceit hurts so much.

A quick look at the train timetable shows there will be one to London in an hour's time. It's the sleeper and will get into Paddington early tomorrow morning. I want to be in a place where I can feel anonymous for a few days and Ashley's dad owns an apartment down at the South Bank.

As I dial Ashley's number, it's hard to keep myself composed.

'Er...Amy? What you doing ringing at this hour?' He sounds sleepy which is hardly surprising given it's getting late.

'Sorry Ashley but I need a favour. Can I use your dad's place in London for a couple of days?'

I give him a garbled explanation about what has happened, promising to put him in the picture properly tomorrow.

'Do you want me to join you?' he asks, his voice a mix of concern and confusion.

No I don't. I need to be on my own but I ask him to ring mum for me, to put her in the picture. He's clearly not too keen.

'Why don't you just text her if you don't want to talk?' He's sounding miffed at my rebuttal of his offer to come down to London.

'Because she won't believe a bloody text. She'll just think someone is using my phone and that I've been kidnapped or something. Knowing her she'll end up phoning the police.'

Ashley sighs and promises to ring her as soon as I've got off the phone.

'I'll ring security at the building to let them know you're coming. You've got the address haven't you?' He sounds less annoyed now, adding that he'll give me 'two days at the most' before he heads down.

'Tell me you won't give mum any details about the place. Just let her know that I'm safe and want some time to think.'

'OK Amy but I'm not happy about what you're asking me to do. You're going to have to sort things out with your mum and I don't want to be dragged into a row between the pair of you.'

'You won't be Ashley but this has come as a massive shock. When I tell you more, you'll understand. Just do this for me now.'

I feel bad about involving Ashley like this but it's for the best. Time now to buy a ticket and head down to the train platform.

I hope mum has the sense not to have called the police before he manages to get hold of her.

Meanwhile, Jemma's text 'please call me' awaits a response.

It's tempting to type in 'f..k off bitch' but where would that get me? It's never good to respond when you're angry and at some point I'll want to talk to her. Find out what the hell my dad was playing at and how long they'd been at it.

I doubt whether it was serious, probably just an older man going through the classic mid-life crisis, trying his luck with a younger model.

For a second I almost feel sorry for mum but the sympathy is fleeting. No, she's kept this to herself, hoping that I'd never find out. It hasn't worked and now I want to confront the whole thing head-on.

For f..k's sake dad, what the hell were you playing at?

My phone bleeps and it's a text from Ashley saying that he's just told mum.

'She was crying down the phone Amy, so why don't you just give her a call?'

I reply straight away.

'No way. She can stew. I'm just getting on the train and I'll phone you when I get to London.'

The place I need to be.

Chapter 30

Back over to me, Debbie, and Ashley's just got off the phone, assuring me that my daughter is all right. He said that she's heading to a place in London owned by his dad.

'Where in London?' I'd demanded, putting him on the spot. Of course he was always going to be loyal to his girlfriend.

'Amy's made me promise not to tell you where but it's a safe area and a secure building. I'll be joining her in a couple of days time - if she's not already back by then.'

'Has she told you what this is all about?' Again, I'm being unfair on him as it's not his problem. He's just caught in the middle of a clunking great pile of muck.

'Not really. She said she'd tell me more later. She just wanted you to know that she's OK, that she just needs to get her head together.'

Ashley can't see that I'm sobbing but I know he can hear it. Try crying silently - it's almost impossible.

'Are you all right Debbie?' I know the poor lad is mortified about having to tell me, so I can hardly be angry with him.

'I'm as fine as I can be Ashley, given my daughter is heading to London and won't answer my calls. Could you ask her again to give me a ring...please?' It's emotional blackmail but what the hell else am I supposed to do?

'I'll ask but I'm not sure she will. You know what Amy's like when she decides to do something.' Yes I do and damn it, she takes after me on that score. What a sodding mess.

As for Kevin, he is trying to be helpful, telling me to let Amy have the space she wants.

'It's been a shock Debbie and she's angry as hell. Just let her be for a bit, she'll come around when it all sinks in.'

There's no point going to bed as I won't sleep a wink. So I tell Kevin to get some shut eye while I try reading to take my mind off things. If only that was a possibility. Instead the next few hours are spent alternately staring into space and sending more texts to Amy 'just in case.' Not a single reply but that doesn't stop me checking the phone every few minutes.

I'm still up when Kevin appears at 6am and it's clear that he hasn't slept much either.

'Did you manage to do some reading?' he asks, knowing already what my answer is going to be. Not a book in sight, just the phone perched on the table and heaven only knows what state my eyes are in.

Getting no response, he puts his arms around me and we stay like that for a while, both lost in our thoughts. Sometimes it really is best just to say '

'I'll put some coffee on.' Kevin's voice jumps in suddenly and I realise just how long we've been holding on to each other. Still, I'm reluctant to let go as he gently kisses my cheek and makes a move to stand up.

'I love you Kevin'. It's not the first time I've told him this but this time I really mean it. Deep down mean it.

'Love you too - panda-eyes and all' he says, ruffling my already unkempt hair. Bless him, he's had to put up with a lot and still manages one of those gorgeous smiles. Kevin you are such a brilliant person and you deserve some happiness in your life. Not this crock of shite that I've just served up to you.

A shower and coffee helps with feeling more human again, as does a text from Ashley confirming that Amy's arrived safely in London. He doesn't add what I know to be the case - that she's still refusing to speak to me.

'Thanks for keeping me posted' I reply, adding that I hope Amy will call back sooner rather than later.

His response is a simple 'x'.

In the wee small hours of this morning, I decided that I was going to approach Jemma to arrange a meeting. Now she's met my daughter, it's time for her to face me as well. Nothing was mentioned to Kevin before he set off for work because he would have tried to put me off. I can hear him now.

'Don't go there. Wait until you've sorted things out with Amy.'

So Jemma. I've heard your voice on an answerphone and now to see you in the flesh. To confront the woman who stole my dead husband's heart and who has thrown a hand grenade slap bang into the middle our lives.

Here we go then - no time like the present.

Chapter 31

Voices - Jemma again...

It's me, Jemma. The day after the evening from hell.

When the office phone rang out, I nearly didn't answer it.

'Is that Jemma Atkins?'

The voice sounded tense, and immediately I began to regret picking it up. I was on my way out to meet a client and already running late. The last thing I needed was a pissed-off customer to make an already crap day even more so.

'Yes Jemma speaking. Can I help you?'

There was an intake of breath before the killer reply.

'My name is Debbie McKay. I believe you knew my husband David.'

Frigging hell. I wasn't expecting that. I glanced around the room to check there was no-one else around. Just me thankfully, everyone else out on the road or ensconced in meetings. At that moment I wished I was with them, far away as possible from this phone and the voice at the end of it.

'Yes, I knew David...er... but I didn't know that he was married to you. Not then anyway.'

I was aware that my voice sounded clipped, harsh even, but that couldn't be helped. I'd been caught literally on the hop and how else could I have responded, other than factually? It was true after all.

'I'd like us to meet' she replied 'sooner rather than later. I gather you've already met my daughter Amy...'

She sounded as wound up as I felt.

'Why do you want to meet?' A really ridiculous question but I could sense her antipathy, someone whose mind had been made up. Me, just a husband – now dead husband – stealing bitch. End of, so what could we possibly have to talk about now?

She didn't reply straight away, hoping no doubt that I'd say something else. But I wasn't playing that game and waited for her response.

'The same reason you want to meet my daughter Jemma again, that's why. She's only just found out about this – my daughter learned through you. I knew but hadn't got round to telling her....'

'Will Amy be there with you?' Already I'd decided that there was no way out of this. We were bound by past events, by David and his deceit. In a way we were all victims, although she and Amy far more so than me.

'No – just you and me to start with. Amy's got enough on her plate already.'

'Where do you want to meet?' In a way, the worst bit of our encounter was over. A one-to-one meeting had to be better than this, the most frigging awkward of phone calls.

She suggested a small coffee bar near Truro Cathedral and we arranged to meet up later that afternoon.

And that was that – cutting straight to the chase, almost business-like. Just how I usually like things but this wasn't something I could control, do up a running order for.

Then I flew out the door before there was a chance of bumping into anyone else. I barely remember the discussion with my client, after I made up a story about being stuck in traffic to cover up for my lateness. I still managed to get a few thousand quids worth of business out of the poor man, but probably not as much as I would have got if my head wasn't full of what to expect later on.

It was still only 12.30pm but no way was I going back into the office. Instead I rang my boss saying that I felt unwell – not entirely without foundation – and was taking the rest of the day off.

'Get a grip Jemma' I whispered to myself as I set off back in the direction of Truro.

All I needed to do was tell the truth, let Debbie know that her husband had been lying to us both. Make her realise that I'd never have got involved with a married man, let alone one with a daughter.

Thing is, will she believe me and would I in her position?

If only we could hook ourselves up to one of those lie detector machines they use on that trashy morning TV programme. Except even they don't always work it seems.

Let's just hope she's got her own mental equivalent of a lie detector. Then again, if she had that ability she might have suspected what her husband was up to.

I wish life was as simple as a machine – red light for 'a husband snatching cow' and green for 'kept in the dark mistress', under the impression that her older boyfriend was a free man.

At least I know the true version.

Chapter 32

The venue I've chosen to meet Jemma is as discreet as it can get for central Truro.

Having arrived early, there's been plenty of time to choose the best seats, as far away from the spewing coffee machine as possible.

My approach has been well thought out. Let her do most of the talking while I weigh her up. Mr DJ would be proud, with me doing exactly as he's suggested. Going on a fact-finding mission, trying to put the missing pieces together. I re-read his last letter again this morning, his advice still resonating in my head.

I still haven't heard anything from Amy and have stopped trying to get her on the phone. As Kevin says, she will sort things out in her own time and then we can sit down and have a proper talk. Woman to woman, as well as mother and daughter.

As the time to meet Jemma approaches, I can feel that familiar nervous knot in my stomach. At least I'm not angry anymore, only with myself for not telling Amy the full story earlier. I was only trying to protect the memory of her dad as a superhero rather than philanderer. As for the other huge secret I'm keeping back from her, well that's yet another dilemma. One step at a time Debbie, let's get this timebomb sorted out first.

When Jemma arrives bang on time, I'm struck by how stressed she looks. No need for cack-handed introductions and as far as I'm concerned this needs to be got over with as quickly as possible, getting straight down to the nitty gritty.

'I'm not here to judge Jemma, but I do want to know all about your relationship with David.'

She nods and I can see that her choice of dress is sober, serious-looking work clothes. A far cry from the sexy in-your-face image I've seen on some of her social networking postings.

'I'm not sure where to start...it all seems so long ago now.' She's toying with her gold chain watch strap, twisting it from side to side. Stay quiet Debbie, remember to let her do the talking.

'It was a conference in Leeds – about 18 months before he died. I'd only been working for the company for a short while and had just had a promotion. '

I nod, trying to look neutral. Mentally I'm flicking back to that time. There were so many work conferences, trips away that they all began to blend into each other. In all honesty, I can barely recall the Leeds conference despite its obvious significance.

'We went to a bar and all got a bit drunk. I was in a flirty mood and had just split up with my boyfriend. David was...well...interesting, not as silly as some of the others. '

Another pause, a tweak of the watch strap. She's looking at me but glances away every time I meet her gaze. Not because she's being shifty, it's more about the sheer awkwardness of the situation.

'We carried on drinking back at the hotel and then I invited a few people to my room for night caps from the mini bar. After a while it was just me and David left...'

'Go on' I say, wanting her to keep going but dreading what I knew to be the next part of the story.

'Then it just sort of happened, you know, we ended up in bed. God Debbie if I'd known he was married...'

I'm desperately trying to get the image of them from my head. Her firm fleshed and gorgeous, him not giving a damn about me or Amy. 'An erect dick knows no conscience' Kevin had once joked, and it seemed funny at the time. Not now though.

'Did you even bother to ask him that evening if he was married or had a partner? I mean did you even care?' I'm coming across as angry, which of course I am, but I'm supposed to be listening, not judging.

'Of course I asked him' Jemma snaps back, her face reddening at the verbal slap she's just received.

'If you must know, he told me that he was separated from his wife a while back and that it had been easier because there were no kids involved.'

My turn to get a verbal rollicking and hell does it hurt. How could David be so damned dismissive of us?

'Sorry Debbie, I know this must be difficult for you to hear but I swear on my own parents lives that it is what he said.' I'm looking closely at her now and she is telling the truth. More facts though Debbie, remember your journalism training.

'You can imagine how hurtful that is for me to hear Jemma, but there's one thing I don't understand. You worked together and a lot of his colleagues knew about me and Amy. How come no-one said anything to you?'

I can tell it's a question she'd already asked herself, once she found out the reality of his life. A discovery made in death.

'Yes, I suppose I could have found out at any time. But if you think about it, I was hardly ever in the office. Most of the time I was on the road and when I did go into work, it was usually for a meeting with David.'

Her face has reddened again, as she guesses correctly what I'm thinking. Please don't say they got intimate at the office as well.

'Before you ask, no we didn't get up to anything at work. At first it was just a bit of fun but then, you know, things started to get more serious. He'd spend the odd weekend at my place and we'd go to his flat sometimes...'

'His flat? What are you talking about?' I'm

thrown by this. How on earth did David have access to a flat?

'The one out in the sticks, near St Agnes. That's where he told me he lived...'

Bloody hell, he must have borrowed a friend's place or rented it out. I'm wracking my brains to think who we knew had a property in that area. St Agnes was a favourite of ours when we first started to go out with each other but it had fallen off the visiting radar a long time before he died. Now I know why.

'But he was living with me and Amy. I've no idea how he managed to get hold of a separate flat.' Hells bells, what else am I going to find out from Jemma?

'Well he did tell me it was his place and he had a lot of stuff there. Clothes and things. He said he was renting it until he could afford somewhere better.'

With my head still spinning from the news of the flat, I'm keen to get back to their relationship and when it started to get more serious.

'About a year in, David bought me a ring – he said it was a 'commitment' symbol. Not an engagement as such....'

I'm looking now at her fingers but there is only one large costume type ring.

'Don't worry I got rid of it as soon as I found out the truth.' It's her turn to glance across at my wedding ring which I'm still wearing. Instinctively I move my hand away, out of her sight.

'I believe these belong to you Jemma. They were hidden away in our garden shed.'

She flinches as I dig out the cards from my bag.

'Here, you might as well have them back. '

'I don't want them' she replies, leaving them sitting on the table.

'They hint that you were planning a holiday together, maybe thinking about buying a place. '

She's clearly taken aback by the cards, and looks distracted.

'Yes, we did talk about a holiday and said if we got on well during the break then we might consider moving in together. But nothing definite had been sorted, it was just talk.'

'Did you love him?' There I've said it. The question has to be asked. For a few moments she looks thoughtful, wistful even.

'We were in love, at least that's what I thought. He was always telling me he loved me, that he was lucky to have me.'

David was the romantic type and barely a day passed by when he didn't tell me and Amy that he loved us. Yet there he was saying the same thing to another woman, all the while thinking of leaving his own family. Unless he was intent on living a double life, like the bizarre stories you read in those tacky 'slice of life' weekly magazines.

'And you never for a moment suspected that he

wasn't hiding something?' As I ask the question, I can see the look of incredulity on her face. If I didn't realise what he was up to, why on earth do I think she should suspect anything? David was clearly an ace liar. Just like his wife in fact, we were two peas in a pod on that score.

'Of course I didn't Debbie. I believed what he told me. I only found out he was married on the day he died – when my senior manager mentioned you and a child. How devastating it must be...'

She's managing to hold everything together, I'll give her that. No sign of tears, even though it must be difficult for her to tell me all of this.

'That's why I didn't go to the funeral service - I couldn't face you and Amy. I only saw you for a few seconds when I hid behind the wall of the church.'

'So you weren't told by any of your workmates that I was the Debbie who worked for Cornwall Now magazine?'

'No, incredible as it may seem, I didn't know you were the same person. I couldn't face going anywhere near the office straight after David's death. I just hid from the world for a while, then resigned and went off travelling.'

I'm still finding it hard to believe that she had a relationship with my husband, was working in a related industry and all the time none of her colleagues ever referred to me or Amy. Yet believe it I must, because it seems to be the case.

Then another thought suddenly springs to mind.

If he did this once, had he done something similar before? It's an idea too unbearable to dwell on.

'And I gather from Amy that you are friends with my boss Carl' I say, trying to push the other stuff to the back of my mind.

I can see that she's wondering how to respond and has reverted to the nervous habit of fiddling with her watch strap.

'Yes, he's a sort of boyfriend. Nothing serious mind, we're both just having some non-committal fun.'

Ah, more than just a friend then.

'Have you told him about any of this?'

'Of course not. Carl doesn't know everything about my past and certainly not that bit.'

'I'd prefer it if you kept it that way Jemma. I don't want Carl feeling sorry for me or for this to affect our working relationship.'

'Don't worry, I'm not planning on telling him anything.'

I nod, signalling to the waiter that I'd like to settle the bill. Also sending out a clear message to Jemma that we're through. For now anyway.

As I get up to leave, she is staring down at the envelopes strewn across the table.

'Keep those or throw them away – it's up to you. Thanks for meeting me though, it can't have been easy.'

She gives me a sort of half smile, a mix of relief and pity.

'Before you go Debbie. What if your daughter gets in touch? I gave her my number.'

'Just tell her to speak to me. I'm going to leave her a message now to say that we've met. Bye.'

I don't wait for Jemma to reply but make straight for the door, grabbing hold of my mobile phone.

Predictably, Amy's answer message kicks in and I come straight to the point.

'Amy, just to let you know that I've met up with Jemma. I really need you to call me back. Please.'

Chapter 33.

Unable and unwilling to return to work, I head home fully expecting Amy to call back this time. I've just met Jemma for heaven's sake, and if I know my own daughter, she'll want to know what was said.

By the time I get home, yet again narrowly avoiding the attentions of old Ted next door, she still hasn't got back. It's surprising but then all this running off to London isn't like her either.

To distract myself, I decide it's time for a reply to Mr DJ's last letter, sent over a month ago. He'll be back from Tenerife by now and I want him to know that I've heeded his advice to confront Jemma. All the time I'm keeping an eye on my mobile phone, ready to pounce if Amy's number shows up.

'Dear Peter,

I hope you had a fantastic time in Tenerife and are settled back in Blighty by the time you read this letter.

First of all, thank you so much for your advice which I've now done something about. More about that anon.

As for those 'secrets', I have to admit that I already knew that you'd lied about your age back then. You've been pretty good about keeping your real age under wraps but I managed to get hold of your date of birth through my cuttings research and documents at Companies House. It came as a surprise but then again, you'll be shocked by my own secret. You see, I wasn't 19 at the time and when we first met I had just finished my 'O' levels. All that stuff about working in the fashion industry was made up. I was only just underage when we first got together but turned 16 only a few weeks later. I know you'll be horrified, especially with all this stuff about 1970s DJ's in the press right now, but trust me I was mature for my age and absolutely knew what I was doing. You mustn't worry on that score although I suspect that you will. Please, please put it to the back of your mind because I don't regret anything from back then and neither should you.

So that's got my own 'secret' out of the way and like you I have other bigger ones which I may take to my grave....'

A pause for another look at the phone. Still no reply from Amy. I hope to God that she doesn't ring Jemma before she speaks to me. I know I've already told Jemma to bat any calls she gets straight in my direction, but what if she ignores my advice?

Back to Mr DJ's letter then.

'....and like you I have other bigger ones which I may take to my grave. Sometimes secrets are best kept that way for a good reason, don't you think?

Now back to the subject of Jemma, the woman who I discovered was having an affair with David before he died. Well we met up for the first time today and like you with your friend, I almost felt sorry for her.

The situation differs from your experience because she

didn't find out that David was married until the day he died. Up to then she thought he was divorced, with no kids to complicate things. I believe her because it fits in with everything else she has said about their relationship.

He'd even taken her to a flat he was renting out or borrowing from someone else. That came as a complete surprise, I can tell you. I already knew from reading Jemma's cards, that they'd been planning to sneak away and it seems that this was to be a test as to whether they should move in together.

I also found out that it had been going on for over a year before he died, so it was a long drawn out deception and it looks like none of their workmates suspected what was really going on between the two of them.

At the moment, I'm confused about the man who was my husband and best friend for so long. To think that he could lead a double life like that without me suspecting a thing.

In your case you sensed something was wrong, whereas I wasn't even looking. Now I'm beginning to wonder if there were other affairs before Jemma came along. Madness, I know, but you can't help thinking.

There's an added complication to this mess. Amy happened to bump into Jemma on a night out – she's just finished a work placement on the magazine and was having a farewell drink with Carl, my boss. Then Jemma turned up – can you believe she's actually now Carl's girlfriend? What a bloody small and messy world.

Anyway, Jemma is talking away to Amy and when she hears her surname, she mentions that she once had a boyfriend called David Mckay. A boyfriend who died four years ago. Of course Amy quickly sussed out what had gone on and then confronted me.

I had no choice but to tell her the truth and now she's flounced off to London. I'm public enemy number one for not letting her know what had been going on between her dad and Jemma – even though I've only recently found out. I've no idea where in London she is, but the boyfriend says that all is well. She just wants to lie low for a few days. As you can imagine, I'm frantic with worry.

I've just left her a message to say that I've spoken to Jemma, so I'm hoping that will do the trick and get her to phone me back. This is the longest I've gone without speaking to her and I just want to hear her voice.

So that's where we are at the moment and you were right about going to meet Jemma. Let's face it, she's also a victim of David's lies and I should feel more sorry for her than I do. It's hard to say from a first meeting, but she comes over as quite steely, self-assured. It can't have been easy to face me but I didn't see any real emotion from her. She might have been putting on a good front – if so, she could get an acting award for her performance.

And now to your suggested theme of hopes and dreams for our children. Before this debacle, I'd have said that I hope Amy gets a good degree and makes her mark in the world. I'd have added that I hope her relationship with Ashley works out well, perhaps even leading to a longer term relationship, marriage and maybe kids. I'd say that I just wanted her to be happy, and hang onto that kind loving personality. To be the grown up version of her lovely self.

Right now my biggest hope is that Amy isn't scarred

for life by this experience, that she doesn't come to hate her dad for what he did. He was her hero and despite everything, I'd like her to hang on to the good memories.

So that's what I hope and dream for her as I write.

Apologies again for a letter that is dealing with personal woes but at least I know you understand.

I'll sign off now with another thank you for all your advice and to remind you not to dwell on the age thing from way back when. We were both only doing what we thought was right for us at the time and I was so touched by your revelation that you had deeper feelings for me than you were prepared to admit then. Of course I had no idea about that but it is so sweet of you to let me know so many years down the line.

Debbie xx

Chapter 34

Voices - Amy again...

Amy here. Sitting tight in this fabulous penthouse apartment with views across the Thames and a bird's eye shot of the hustle and bustle that is London.

It's been great to just sit and watch the world go by, wondering about the life stories behind the passing people below. Where are they heading? What thoughts are swirling through their minds? Does the day ahead promise happiness or great sadness?

Mum has been leaving messages and texting constantly. I know she's worried but Ashley has told her that I'm fine. I suppose I'll have to ring back soon but for now I'm happy to bask in the silence of this place, hovering miles above the mayhem below.

Ashley's joining me here tomorrow and after two days of solitude, I'll be happy to see him. He wants us to go out for a meal – 'you must be going stir crazy by now' – he told me on the phone last night. But I'd prefer to stay in here, cosy up in front of an escapist film and order in his favourite Chinese food. Just the two of us, snuggling up against the mad outside world.

I can hear that another text has just come in and it's probably from Ashley, letting me know which train he'll be on. He'll be travelling First Class of course, like he usually does. Occasionally he's slummed it in 'standard class' - or 'coach' as they say in America – just to humour me. A bit like that 'Pulp' song about 'common people.' It's easy to pretend at being poor when you've got a trust fund and rich family behind you. Ashley will never know what it is like not to have choices and of course, I'm benefitting from that right now.

The words in the text jump out, a complete surprise.

'Amy, just to let you know that I've met up with Jemma. I really need you to call me back. Please.'

Short and sweet this time, no blackmail about being worried sick and needing to explain. Mum's finally got my attention.

I want to ring straight back but hold off. If I 'fess up' to use one of Ashley's favourite expressions, then I'd have to admit to missing mum. The sound of her voice, the smell of her favourite perfume, her bad jokes.

Then again, I'm reminded of that other mother, the one I don't recognise. The one who keeps things back from her daughter, important things. The one who allows her daughter to find out these from a complete stranger. Things about her dad.

Things. Terrible things.

The anger and hurt is starting to get a bit less, at least towards mum. Today it's dad I'm pissed off with, inwardly railing at him as if he were still alive.

Last night I dreamt that he was here and that he'd managed to track me down. At first I was overjoyed to see him, drinking in his familiar form and silly lopsided smile. Then I started yelling, punching hard at him with my fists. Why did he have to betray us? What the f..k was he even thinking about, screwing around like some sad cliché of a middle-aged crisis? I woke up angry, my hands clenched and mouth dry. 'Bastard.' I muttered under my breath and boy, did I mean it.

I'm re-reading mum's text. 'I've met up with Jemma.'

Shit, I'm going to have to get back. If curiosity really did kill the cat, it sure as hell will do it to me. Mum, you've won on this one, with your pithy no nonsense message.

1, 2, 3... here we go.

Time for Jemma's big reveal. And to break this deadly silence.

In more ways than one.

Chapter 35

'It's me mum. And before you say anything, I just want to hear what Jemma said. That's the only reason I've rung you.'

I'm stung by her rudeness, the defensiveness of her voice.

'Are you all right Amy? I been worried...'

'Jemma mum. Forget about me, I'm fine.'

It doesn't sound like my lovely Amy, there's a harshness that I don't recognise. She sounds tense, a tightly coiled spring. Then again, so am I. Like mother, like daughter as they say.

'All right, have it your way. I rang Jemma at work this afternoon and arranged to meet her at the Lime Tree coffee shop.'

I pause for a moment, waiting for Amy to react. But there is nothing, just the sound of her light breathing and a sense of her impatience for me just to get on with it.

'I found out that she'd been in a relationship with your dad for over a year before he died. They would meet in a flat in St Agnes and he told her it was his place. He said that he'd split up from me, that he didn't have kids...'

Another pause as I give her a few seconds to take in what I've just said.

Still no response, so I plough on.

'None of their work colleagues knew and just before your dad died, they'd been planning to go away together...'

Amy cuts in, and I can hear the shock and hurt in her voice.

'So he was going to leave us then...?'

'I don't know Amy and we'll never find out now. Maybe he was just stringing her along, giving her the impression that they might move in together.'

Amy's breathing seems to have got more laboured. Or is she crying?

'Sorry if I'm upsetting you darling. There's no easy way of telling you this...'

'I'm just angry mum. What sort of dad would deny that he had a kid and pretend he was divorced? It's not the dad I knew - or thought I knew more like.'

I want to give Amy a big hug, to tell her that despite everything, her dad had many good sides. But I know deep down that there is no point in saying it.

'And you mum – exactly how long have you known about this?'

She's batted the ball back to my court, deflecting from the hurt inflicted by David.

'You know Amy, I tried to tell you the other evening.' I find myself repeating the story about the stash of cards secreted in our old garden shed, something I discovered just a few months ago.

'Yet you didn't even think to say anything? I mean, what's with the big cover up? We never have secrets, not until now anyway.'

Oh Amy. That bit I wish I could say was true. We have secrets all right. Deeper ones which may still need to come out.

Before I can answer her question, Amy sideswipes me with another.

'Dad can't have been happy if he was seeing Jemma on the side can he?'

It's something I've been thinking long and hard about for months. She's right though, he can't have been happy.

'Amy darling, I'd no idea things were not going well. I mean there were no obvious signs...'

'Come on, he was hardly ever at home towards the end mum. Always off working somewhere or other. I guess that's when he was seeing this Jemma. Still, if he was happy he wouldn't have done it.'

Hurtful but true.

'What's it going to be now mum? I mean we can't just leave this, burying our heads in the sand, pretending everything is fine. I don't recognise my parents any more...'

She's definitely crying now, I can hear the sobs in her voice and there's nothing I can do to make things better.

Yet Amy, in her young direct way, has reinforced a valuable life lesson. Secrets have a habit of coming out, worming their way through to the surface, breaking through when you least expect it.

I'm exhausted with trying to pretend, putting a sticking plaster on things that need to have fresh air and light.

No more. The time has finally come to tell my daughter the truth. Not just about her dad but about her brother Andy as well. Everything, no holds barred.

'Amy, listen to me. I really do need you to come home. We need to have a serious talk as I've got a lot more to tell you. It's not something I want to discuss over the phone.'

She sniffs, aware of the marked change in my voice. This isn't a request, damn it. It's an order, an important one.

'OK, I'll come home with Ashley the day after tomorrow. But mum – no more hiding things. Whatever else you've got to say, I'm big enough to take it. Right?'

'No more secrets Amy – promise.'

I'm just about to add that 'I love you' when she

hangs up the phone.

No more, I said. Promise, I said.

Please God don't let this be the point where I lose my daughter, having just regained a son.

The next mother and daughter talk will be the most important of our lives. Everything will change and that's what scares me the most.

Time to throw away that old festering sticking plaster. It's been hanging around for far too long.

Right now though I need some sage grown-up advice, to prepare myself for the emotional tsunami I'm about to unleash.

But this time it won't be from my partner Kevin. Nor from Liverpool Lil my adoption adviser. Neither will it come from my son Andy or his lovely parents and certainly not from Mr DJ.

No, there's only one person I want to turn to and he's a virtual stranger.

A man called Philippe Roux.

To be continued - see what happens next in the third book of the 'Dilemma Novella' trilogy.

Now that you have read this novella, would you consider writing a review? Reviews are the best way for readers to discover new books and will be much appreciated.

And if you enjoyed this novella then do try the first book of the trilogy, 'Dear Mr. DJ', my novel, 'My Bermuda Namesakes', or my short story 'Key' . See details and reviews on websites www.maggiefogarty.com and www.amazon.co.uk/www.amazon.com.

About the Author:

Maggie Fogarty is a Royal Television Society award winning television producer and journalist, making TV programmes for all the major UK broadcasters. She has also written extensively for a number of national newspapers and magazines.

In April 2011 her story 'Namesakes' was a finalist in the Writers and Artists/WAYB short story competition.

'My Bermuda Namesakes' was her debut novel and grew out of the original short story. It was written during a year long stay in Bermuda where Maggie's husband, Paul, was working as a digital forensics consultant. During her time on the island, Maggie wrote a guest column for the Bermuda Sun newspaper.

'Dilemmas and Decisions' is Maggie's second novella and forms part of a trilogy called the 'Dilemma Novellas'.

Maggie and her husband now live Cornwall in the far South West of England with their cockapoo dog Bonnie. Before moving there, they lived on the outskirts of Birmingham, in the English Midlands, where Maggie was born and grew up.

Author website: www.maggiefogarty.com